A Love for Lexi

Love will OUT #7

D.E. Haggerty

Also By D.E. Haggerty

A Hero for Hailey
A Protector for Phoebe
A Fox for Faith
A Soldier for Suzie
A Christmas for Chrissie
A Valentine for Valerie
My Forever Love
Forever For You
Just For Forever
Stay For Forever
Only Forever
Meet Disaster
Meet Not
Meet Dare
Meet Hate
Bragg's Truth
Bragg's Love
Perfect Bragg
About Face
At Arm's Length

Hands Off
Knee Deep
Molly's Misadventures

Chapter 1

The difference between a girlfriend and a girl friend is the space in between we call a 'friend zone'.

WHACK! I GRUNT WHEN the bridal bouquet hits me smackdab in the face. I watch as it falls to the floor. I could catch it, but I'm not going to, because I – Lexi Mullins – have no intention of being a bride, thank you very much.

The current bride, Faith, points to the bouquet and yells, "It's your turn next!"

At her words, a cheer rises up from the crowd. They can cheer all they want. It doesn't change a thing. Love is not for this woman. I've learned my lesson.

It's past time to escape, but I don't have a chance to stand before Lenny appears in front of me. Great. Another situation I don't want to deal with. The man refuses to understand the term 'friend zone' no matter how many times I explain it to him.

But boy, oh boy is the man pretty to ogle. I fist my hands to stop from fanning myself at all the glory that is Lenny looming above me. The man may be over fifty but he's still sexy as all get out. He has dark brown eyes I can't seem to look away from, laugh lines around his eyes that tell me he enjoys a good time, and a dimple in his chin I want to lick while I scratch his always present five o'clock shadow.

He's also several inches over six-foot-tall, and his clothes are covering up a whole bunch of muscles. Trust me. I know. For one delicious moment on New Year's Eve, my hands roamed all over those muscles.

Unfortunately – ahem, I mean, fortunately – my mind overruled my body and reminded me of how all his friends and my friends are intertwined. Which is a dang shame. If they weren't, I'd take him for a test drive with no intention of buying. Alas, things would get way too complicated way too quickly, and I can't do complicated. Not yet, at least.

"Not now, Lenny," I tell him before he can open his mouth.

I'm not blowing smoke up his ass – no matter how much I'd love to. Now is really not the time to discuss our non-relationship. This is a wedding. Weddings are for watching the newly married couple look disgustingly happy – gag – and laughing at all the single bridesmaids getting drunk and hitting on the single groomsmen.

Considering this wedding is happening on Valentine's day, I would normally expect the single bridesmaids to jump on any single man in this place before the nuptials have even been spoken. Which would be absolutely hilarious to observe. But there's one problem. Lenny and I are the only unattached people in the room. Even the bride's son has a girlfriend.

Lenny ignores my warning – what's new? – and leans over to place his hands on the back of my chair. He thinks he's got me blocked in. Silly man. He forgets who I am and where I come from. Also, I don't fight fair.

"Doll."

I roll my eyes. He calls everyone doll. He doesn't seriously believe I think he's treating me special when he calls me the same endearment he uses for every other woman in his life, does he? How stupid does he think I am?

"When are you going to stop fighting our attraction, Lexi?"

I snort. "Um, never. Friend zone, remember? Do you need for me to explain it to you again?"

"You can't fight our attraction forever."

"Never going to happen." Judging by the heads turning in our direction, I must have yelled. Oopsie.

"It is," he growls.

My insides quiver, and my middle tingles at the sound. I ignore my body's response. It's not running the show here. I am.

"Dream on." I shove him out of my way before standing and marching away.

I make my way to the restroom, but I'm ambushed before I can open the door. My friend, Chrissie, stands blocking me with her arms crossed over her chest. I step back and slam into a different body. I whirl around to find another friend, Hailey, barring my escape route. Behind her stands the rest of the girl crew. Aka Suzie, Phoebe, Val, and Mary Ann.

"Goodie. The gang's all here."

Faith comes rushing down the hallway. "Wait for me."

Correction. Now, the gang's all here.

I'm still not convinced about this group of women. Except for Chrissie, I've only known them since I showed up on Christmas Day for Chrissie's surprise wedding. She wasn't the only one surprised. I didn't know the woman was dating anyone, let alone ready to legally attach herself to a man. But her boyfriend, Wally, called me and told me to get my butt to Milwaukee if I wanted to be at my best friend's wedding.

When I hopped on the plane in D.C., I didn't believe for a minute Chrissie was getting married. I assumed the call was some part of an ambush. There was an ambush all right. Just not the kind requiring guns and grenades. Instead, Wally surprised Chrissie with a wedding on Christmas Day.

Chrissie grabs my arm and frog marches to the office. She throws the door open like she owns McGraw's Pub. She doesn't. The bride's husband, Max, owns the pub, which is why the wedding took place in a bar of all places.

As soon as I hear the door of the office click closed, I whirl around on the women. "What is wrong with you people?"

Phoebe raises her hand. "I'm pregnant, my feet are swollen, and I feel nauseous all the time."

Suzie frowns at her. "She didn't mean literally."

"I did," I say. Mostly, to hear what Suzie's response is. The woman is crazy. The fun kind of crazy. Not the 'I have to kill her to save the world'– kind. I'm finished with those kind since I quit my job.

"Oh, in that case, same as whiny girl here. Except for the nauseous thing. I'm over it."

Mary Ann, who happens to be a nurse, asks Phoebe, "How far along are you? If you continue to feel nauseous, maybe you should discuss it with your OB/GYN."

With the women distracted discussing pregnancy, I decide it's time to take my leave. I've got the door open and one foot in the hallway when Chrissie stops me.

"And where do you think you're going?"

I shrug. "Back to the party."

A champagne cork pops, and Val waves a bottle in the air. "But the party is in here now. Don't leave me here alone. The pregnant women can't drink."

Hailey's hand shoots into the air. "I'm not pregnant."

While Val pours glasses of champagne, I decide to try and sneak off again. Once more, I don't make it far. Chrissie grunts before stomping to me, grabbing my upper arm, and dragging me back into the room. "It's time for you to fess up."

I raise an eyebrow. "Fess up? About what?"

She already knows I quit my job. I have no other secrets to tell. My phone in my pocket beeps with a message. Okay, maybe I have one more secret she doesn't know about.

"I vote we let this play out," Hailey says.

Suzie snorts. "Yeah, because today's your day."

I widen my eyes and pretend I don't know what's going on. "What are you talking about?"

"Don't act as if you don't know," Chrissie mutters.

Of course, I know. These women haven't exactly made a secret of how they're betting on when Lenny and I will burn up the sheets.

Mary Ann giggles. "Have I mentioned lately how much I love all of you?"

Val lifts her glass. "Here. Here."

"Can we get this over with?" Faith asks. "I want to get back to my groom."

I motion to the door. "By all means."

She doesn't move. "Not before you tell us what's going on with you and Lenny."

If you read the entry for 'nosy' in the dictionary, you'll find a picture of this group. I thought my family was nosy, but they can't hold a candle to these people.

"There's nothing to tell."

Hailey crosses her arms over her chest. "Really? Why was he caging you in your chair?"

"And why did he look like you stole his puppy when you walked away?" Val adds.

I place a hand on my chest and gasp. "I would never steal a puppy."

Chrissie shoves everyone out of the way to stand in front of me. Her hands fist at her hips as if she's preparing for battle.

"The quicker you answer our questions, the quicker you can return to the party."

I place my hand on my chest and feign a tremble. "The big bad intimidating interrogator has arrived. I'm scared." For good measure, I curl my button lip out in a pout.

Chrissie's hands drop and her shoulders slump. "You're one of my oldest friends. Why won't you tell me what's going on?"

I'm surprised she doesn't wipe at her eyes as if tears are forming. There's more than one way to interrogate a suspect after all. And Chrissie is an expert in all of the methods. I know this for a fact. We used to work together. While I was an analyst who kept my butt firmly imprinted on a chair behind a computer, Chrissie was out in the field doing all kinds of things that would give most people nightmares.

I decide to give in. I need to get out of this room before I fall for one of Chrissie's interrogation methods and accidentally spill my secrets.

"There's nothing going on between Lenny and me." Before I can finish, everyone's shouting out their disbelief. I hold up my hand to cut them off.

"I'm serious. Lenny is in the friend zone. And it's where he's going to stay."

Chrissie taps her chin as she studies me. I keep my face blank and wait. After thirty incredibly long seconds, a smile breaks out on her face.

"This is going to be fun."

I don't wait for whatever else she has to say. The smile is my get out of jail free card and I'm not wasting it. I open the door and hightail it away from the women.

Chapter 2

The only person you should try to be better than
is your best friend.

I GRIN WHEN I open the door to find Chrissie standing on the porch in her workout clothes. She can beat me in most things, but I can kick her ass on a long run any day of the week and twice on Sunday. And, lucky me, today's Sunday.

"You ready to get your ass kicked?" I ask as I exit the house and close the door behind me.

"It's weird having you live here," she says, and I come to a halt.

"What? You don't want me here?"

"Did you hurt yourself jumping to that conclusion without warming up?"

I cross my arms over my chest. "Ha ha. You literally said it's weird having me live here. What am I supposed to think?"

"It's Wally's house. Of course, it's weird having my friend live in it."

Oh yeah. I'm renting her husband's house. "Considering the weird shit I found in his shed, I get it."

She leans close. "What weird shit?"

I shove her away. "I'm not telling you, freak."

Her bottom lip juts out. "Please. Pretty please."

Spoiler alert: I didn't find a thing in the shed. Seriously, it's been completely cleared out. But what's the fun in telling her the truth? I ignore her to lean over and stretch until I can reach my toes. After I count to ten, I pop back up and start jogging in place.

"Come on. Let's get going. I haven't got all day."

I do have all day. I have nothing to do. I'm stuck in limbo. I no longer have a job consuming my life. I thought I'd enjoy having some free time, but free time is overrated. I've cleaned Wally's house from head to toe – including behind the refrigerator. And if moving a three-hundred-pound machine isn't an indication of how bored I've been, I don't know what is.

Chrissie catches my arm before I can sprint off the porch. "We're not going for a run."

My brow wrinkles. "We're not? Please tell me we aren't going to Sunday brunch dressed in our workout clothes."

"No, silly. What we're going to do is way more fun than stuffing our faces."

"Promises. Promises."

We jump in Chrissie's car, and she drives us fifteen minutes to an industrial complex.

"What's this?" I ask as we gather in front of her car.

"This is where I'm going to show you who's boss."

"In your dreams, Chrissie Lindberg."

She elbows me. "It's Nelson now."

Of course, I know she took on Wally's last name. I also know it bugs the heck out of her when I use her maiden name. And pushing her buttons is too much fun. As is kicking her ass at whatever this is we're going to do. I might be a tad bit competitive in nature.

It's why Chrissie and I are such good friends. She's also competitive with a capital C. A lot of people are turned off by competitiveness. Not me. On the first day of training, Chrissie nearly fainted while trying to beat some guy in a push-up competition. When she collapsed, I held out my hand to help her up. We've been friends ever since.

We enter the building, and I study the interior. It appears to be some sort of obstacle course similar to the one from our training except there are mats on the floor if you fall. A luxury no government obstacle course would dare have.

"It's parkour," Chrissie explains.

"Thanks, Captain Obvious."

I've never done parkour before, but I've seen it online. And then there was the one time I got stuck in some tiny village on an island in Greece when they were holding the World Championships. Old world narrow cobble streets and world championships do not go together. Although, I didn't mind being stuck when I was 'forced' to console the man who came in tenth place.

I elbow her. "What are you going to give me when you lose, loser?"

"Loser buys lunch."

I stick out my hand. Before she can shake it, I add, "And is driving to lunch so I can get my drink on."

"It's on," Chrissie agrees.

We do a few stretching exercises before gathering at the start of the course. "Whoever finishes the course first wins."

"Gotcha."

I rub my hands together. This is going to be fun. Chrissie may be the field operative whereas I'm the desk jockey, but guess who hasn't had anything to do but work out for the past month and a half? Hint – it's me. I am so going to kick her ass.

We ask the manager to start us off. He rolls his eyes and mumbles under his breath about hating those military types. Ha! We're not military. We're way more dangerous.

"Ready. Set. Go!"

I'm off before the word 'go' is finished. I jump up to the high bar and swing myself forward to the block with Chrissie right next to me.

"So," I say as we hop to the next block. "I hear Wally has a tiny dick."

She sputters and promptly falls off the block. "Cheater!"

All's fair in love and war. She should know this. She's been to enough war-torn countries.

I scramble to the low wall and swing over it. Her jab rings out as my legs are flying through the air. "At least I'm not on the longest dry spell in history."

Does she think her words will make me stumble? I know I'm on the longest dry spell ever experienced by any woman in the history of womankind. Except for nuns. Although I'm not convinced those nuns in the middle ages were all purity and innocence. Some of them had been married after all.

We continue taunting each other for the next fifteen minutes as we finish the course. When I'm nearing the finish line, I feel Chrissie tugging at my t-shirt.

"Cheater!" I cry as I remove the shirt and cross the finish line in my sports bra.

"Damn. I forget you're not a prude. I thought everyone from West Virginia was a prude."

I grunt. She's been to visit my family during the holidays. She knows there's nothing prudish about my family. Crazy? We have the crazy gene in spades. But prudes? Nope. None of those to be found.

"Let's make it two out of three."

I grin. She's such a bad loser. "You're on."

I laugh as I watch Chrissie cringe as she oh so slowly takes her seat across from me at the diner. Her tailbone is bruised, and I feel zero amounts of guilt about it. She was the one who thought she could hop over to my block and push me off of it.

"You're way meaner than you used to be," Chrissie mutters as she picks up the menu.

"I'm not the one who decided to turn parkour into a full body combat sport."

She snarls at me, and I giggle. I forgot how much fun Chrissie is to be around. Although, we didn't see a whole lot of each other in the past. While I sat at my desk in Langley, she was usually off in countries most people can't pronounce the names of let alone know exist.

"Listen," she says as she sets her menu down. "I have something I want to discuss with you."

I hold up my hand. "If this is about Lenny, I don't want to hear it."

My body hears the word Lenny and thinks about his soft lips and how they felt on mine. How they felt as he kissed his way down my neck to my shoulder. I shiver before I can stop myself.

Chrissie smirks. "I wasn't talking about Lenny but you're definitely thinking about him."

"Whatever."

The waitress interrupts to ask for our order. I use the time to strengthen my defenses. Lenny is a friend, I remind myself. I can't have him. My phone beeps and reminds me there's a reason I'm being bullheaded with regard to the man.

Once we're alone again, Chrissie clears her throat. "I actually do have a serious matter to discuss with you."

My mouth drops open. "Oh my god, you're pregnant."

She throws her napkin at me. "I'm forty-nine years old, I'm not pregnant. You know what they say about making assumptions …"

"Yeah, yeah. I'm an ass. What's this serious matter you want to discuss?"

What could possibly be serious? My phone beeps again. Oh yeah. That could be a serious matter. But Chrissie doesn't know about it. Or does she? I narrow my eyes and study her. She doesn't appear to be about to admit she knows all my secrets.

"I'm quitting my job," she announces.

Huh. This is not where I saw this conversation going. "Why? I thought you loved working at *You Cheat, We Eat*."

You Cheat, We Eat is the PI firm Hailey and Suzie founded. Suzie thought her boyfriend was cheating on her and asked Hailey to find out if her worry was warranted. Hailey discovered she had the skills to be a PI – probably because her 'uncles' are all former military who thought helping raise her meant teaching her how to hotwire cars and break into houses – and thus *You Cheat, We Eat* was born. FYI – Suzie's ex was a total cheater, cheater pumpkin eater.

"If I have to spend another day sitting behind a computer, I'm going to lose my mind." I cock an eyebrow. "No offense intended."

I glare at her for a moment longer. I'm not offended, but I'd be remiss in my friend duties if I didn't give her a hard time whenever the opportunity presents itself.

I sigh – long and hard. "It's okay. I guess."

Chrissie reaches across the table and squeezes my hand. "I'm sorry."

I try to hold onto my upset face for a moment longer, but I can't. A giggle escapes me. Chrissie drops my hand before leaning back in her booth and crossing her arms over her chest.

"You're a pain in my ass."

I wiggle my eyebrows. "Literally."

"Can you be serious for a moment?" I shrug. I can. Will I choose to? Jury's still out. "I want to know if you're interested in being the office manager at *You Cheat, We Eat*."

I freeze. This conversation took a turn I wasn't expecting. "I don't know if I'm in Milwaukee for the long haul."

It's the truth. I came to Milwaukee because Chrissie's here, and I had nowhere else to go. My phone vibrates in my pocket. Correction. Nowhere else I want to go.

"No one's asking you to sign a twenty-year contract. Will you at least consider it?"

I nod. I don't exactly have any plans for my future anyway.

"Good. Your interview is tomorrow at nine."

Her grin says she thinks she pulled a fast one on me. Whatever. After I thoroughly whooped her ass this morning, I'll let this one go. I can be generous like that.

Chapter 3

You don't have to be crazy to be my friend. I'll
train you.

I ENTER THE offices of *We Cheat, You Eat* at exactly 9 a.m. the next day. I may have not made up my mind yet about whether I'm staying in Milwaukee, but there's no harm in checking out where Chrissie works.

I smile as I scan the area. It has gumshoe detective written all over it. The reception area has a large beaten-up desk Chrissie is sitting behind with two worn chairs in front of it. There are four doors off of the main area. Two of the four doors are half milk glass with names etched on them. The other two have stickers indicating they're the storage room and restroom. Add in the wood paneling on the walls and the scuffed floors, and I feel as if I've traveled back in time to the 1950s.

The door behind Chrissie's desk – the one with Hailey's name etched on it – opens up and two dogs rush out. One dog aims straight for me while the other one sniffs and scratches while whining at the door with Phoebe's name etched on it.

"Is it bring your pet to work day?" I ask as I scratch the dog's ears.

Chrissie huffs. "No one lets me bring Gray to work."

Hailey snorts as she joins us. "Yeah, because having a kitten around two dogs is such a great idea."

"Is it time?" Phoebe says as she opens her door. She sees the dog, and her eyes widen as she retreats a step. "No, Lola. Leave me alone."

Chrissie sighs before whistling for the dog. The dog howls before dropping to her belly.

"You need to teach me how to whistle," Phoebe says.

A chair squeaks and heavy footfalls approach her before her husband, Ryker, wraps an arm around her and draws her near. "You don't need to learn to whistle. Hailey needs to send her dogs to obedience school."

Before Hailey can respond, the door behind me crashes open and Suzie rushes in. "I'm here. Am I late?"

"We haven't started yet," Hailey tells her.

I can't help myself, I have to ask. "Started what?"

Suzie claims the chair next to me. "Your interview, silly."

"I get why they," I sweep my arm out to indicate Hailey, Phoebe, and Ryker, "are part of the interviewing thing, but why are you?"

Suzie used to be the office manager of the PI firm she founded with Hailey until Chrissie took over her job. Now, she's entirely too busy operating her microbrewery with her husband, Grayson, to work here. Apparently, brewing was a side gig until the ex-Army guy appeared in her life. He's some kind of marketing guru, and her brewery took off under his tutelage.

"As long as you're willing to answer the phone for me and do my invoicing, I don't need to be part of this," Ryker says.

Ryker isn't a PI. He's a bounty hunter. He actually met Phoebe when he was hired by her ex-husband to find her and bring her home. He ended up falling in love with her instead, and Phoebe's first husband is now in prison for kidnapping her. I don't know all the details, but from what I have heard it's a long and complicated story.

"I can answer your phone and do your invoicing," I say when Ryker stares at me as if his words were actual questions.

At six-foot-six with a big, bushy beard, Ryker's appearance is kind of scary, but he doesn't scare me. I don't scare easily. My phone vibrates in my pocket calling me a liar.

Ryker nods at me before kissing Phoebe's forehead and returning to his desk. Phoebe and Ryker must share an office. The beautiful woman dressed in designer clothes is a PI, too. I know. I couldn't believe it either when I heard. And, yes, I know I'm judging a book by its cover, but my job for some twenty-plus years was to judge people. Only we called it analyzing, not judging.

"Shall we begin?" I ask when no one speaks after Ryker returns to his desk.

Hailey props herself on Chrissie's desk. "This isn't an actual interview."

My brow wrinkles. "It's not? I thought you needed to find a replacement for Chrissie."

Hailey frowns at Chrissie. "We do, because apparently, someone wants to be a PI, but not work for this business."

"Wait. What?" Suzie asks. "I thought you were quitting to spend more time playing with Wally's bed snake."

Phoebe shivers. "Bed snake? It doesn't slither and bite."

Suzie winks at her. "But it does spit venom."

Ryker's chair squeaks before he marches out of his office. He kisses Phoebe's forehead and leaves without another word spoken. I stare after him wondering if he'll let me tag along to wherever he's going.

"Phew. We got rid of Ryker. Now we can get down to the nitty-gritty." Huh. Suzie isn't the floozy she plays. Duly noted. "Did you and Lenny do the horizontal mambo yet?"

Hailey rubs her hands together. "Big money. Big money."

"Sorry to disappoint, but Lenny and I are just friends."

"Damn it. I was positive I would win this bet with the way Lenny was staring at you with big cartoon hearts in his eyes."

As if. "The man is in his fifties. He doesn't have big cartoon hearts in his eyes."

"Wrong." Hailey makes a loud buzzer sound. "Pops is in his fifties, and he totally has big cartoon hearts in his eyes when he stares at Faith."

"Stop!" Phoebe shouts. "Do not talk about your dad and Faith."

"I don't know what the big deal is. They're both consenting adults."

Phoebe glares at Hailey. "There is something seriously wrong with you."

I ignore them to ask Chrissie, "Is this what it's like working here all the time? Maybe I don't want to interview after all."

"I told you," Hailey interrupts to say. "This isn't an interview."

"Color me confused. Did you change your mind, Chrissie?" I smirk. "Or do you plan to fail the PI exam?"

Chrissie rolls her eyes at me. "As if I've ever failed anything in my life."

Really? As if thinking your ex-boyfriend who happened to be a wanted man is dead and not a danger to the entire freaking world isn't a failure. I stare at her in disbelief, and she snaps her teeth at me.

"Oh, my dog." Suzie jumps to her feet and points at me. "You know Chrissie's secret."

I don't dignify her comment with a response. Of course, I know Chrissie's secret. Duh. Former work colleague turned friend.

When I don't speak, Suzie bats her eyelashes at Hailey. "You need to get Lexi drunk and get her to spill the beans."

I lean back in my chair. "This should be fun."

My family are moonshiners. I've been drinking the stuff since I was old enough to stand on my own two feet. No one – except maybe my cousin Jeremy – can out drink me. They're welcome to try, though. It's always fun watching people fail.

Hailey snorts. "Have you met Lexi? I'll be passed out hugging a bottle of tequila before she gets a buzz on."

"True story," Chrissie murmurs.

As much as I find the banter among the women amusing, we need to get this show on the road. I don't need them digging into my past any more than they already are.

"Are we going to do this interview or what?" I ask like I have somewhere to be. Hint: I don't.

"I already told you – this isn't an interview. You've got the job," Hailey claims before rubbing her hands together. "Everyone's here because we want to know what's going on with you and Lenny."

I sigh. "Didn't we have this conversation less than forty-eight hours ago?"

"A lot can happen in forty-eight hours," Phoebe says.

"Hell yeah, it can." Suzie rubs her belly making it obvious what she's thinking about. Although, it's not hard to know since the woman is always making sexual innuendos.

"The only thing to happen in the last forty-eight hours is I kicked Chrissie's ass in parkour."

Hailey's jaw drops open. "You?" She points at me. "Kicked her ass?" She points at Chrissie.

"She cheated," Chrissie answers before I have a chance to.

"You're the one who grabbed hold of my t-shirt, so I had to cross the finish line without a top on."

Suzie wiggles her eyebrows. "I bet Lenny wishes he'd been there to see."

I breathe deeply and reign in my temper. I know she's trying to get me to admit to being with Lenny. Too bad for her the truth is Lenny and I are merely friends. It doesn't matter if he wants more. I don't. End of discussion.

"I wouldn't have had to grab hold of your shirt if you hadn't pushed me off the block."

"I didn't push you. You fell."

Chrissie glares at me. "It was your fault. You disparaged Wally's manhood."

"Disparaged? Manhood?" I snort. "How old are you again?"

"The same age as you, so don't go making ageist comments."

Phoebe's eyes widen as she looks between us. "Holy cow. They're Hailey and Suzie except two decades older."

As one, Chrissie and I turn our gazes on Phoebe. "We are not two decades older than Hailey and Suzie!" We shout in unison.

Phoebe buries her face in her hands. "I'm surrounded by crazy people."

"As if you aren't your own brand of crazy, Pheebs," Suzie claims.

"I am not crazy," she denies.

"Can we talk salary and benefits?" I ask Hailey before the two pregnant women can get into a hairpulling fight.

"If you're going to talk about boring stuff, I'm out of here," Suzie says and picks up her purse to leave.

"You're the one who majored in business administration at college," Hailey calls after her.

"I'm seriously reconsidering this job. I don't know if I can handle being surrounded by crazy people all day."

Chrissie cocks a brow. "I don't know why not. They remind me of your family."

Her words must have conjuring power as my phone vibrates again. At this point, I'm considering going analog and throwing the stupid thing in Lake Michigan.

Chapter 4

Never let your friends be lonely.... Disturb them all the time.

LENNY

I whistle as I stroll up the sidewalk to Wally's old house where Lexi is currently living. She's going to be pissed I showed up without calling first, but I know better than to give her advance warning to allow her to shore up her defenses.

"Just a sec," Lexi shouts after I knock on her door.

The door flies open a minute later and there she is. The woman I'm determined to make mine. She's utterly gorgeous with her light-brown hair pulled up in a high ponytail allowing me a view of the long neck I want to lick and bite. Her light-brown eyes remind me of the color of my favorite whiskey, and her slightly upturned nose does this adorable crinkle thing whenever she's annoyed at me.

My eyes travel downward to examine the rest of her. She's wearing a t-shirt highlighting her perky breasts and jeans that appear to have been painted on her long legs. Legs I can't wait to have wrapped around me. I clear my throat and force those thoughts away.

Lexi claims there's nothing more than friendship between us. It's cute she thinks I'm going to not fight for more.

"I brought pizza." I lift up the box as proof.

Her nose scrunches. "What are you doing here?"

I don't wait for an invitation. I force my way past her into the house. I survey the place, but the interior appears to be exactly the same as when Wally lived here. I expected colorful blankets or pillows – some kind of girly stuff to indicate she lives here – but there's nothing. I file the information away for later perusal.

"I thought you might want to have some pizza and watch a movie." I pause. "Because we're friends."

At the word friends, the tension in Lexi's body releases, and she shuts the door behind her. I dip my chin to hide my grin from her. This is going to be fun.

"What kind of pizza did you get?"

"Sausage and mushrooms."

She feigns gagging. "Vegetables on pizza? What is wrong with you? Did your daddy not love you?"

I shrug. "Probably not seeing as he left when I was a baby."

Her eyebrows shoot off her forehead and she smacks a hand in front of her mouth. "Oh, my dog. I'm sorry."

I pause a second. "I'm teasing you. I had a great dad."

Her hand falls away from her mouth, and she slaps me on the shoulder. "No joking about family."

I chuckle. "You fell for it."

She rolls her eyes. "Because I don't know anything about your family."

I set the pizza down on the kitchen island and open my arms wide. "Ask me whatever you want, Whiskey. My life's an open book." At least, for her it is.

She snorts. "No thanks. I don't need to hear about all your sexual escapades, man whore."

I ignore the sting her words cause. "Hey! That's Sergeant Man Whore to you."

She whips out a salute. "Yes, sir. Whatever you say, sir."

I wrap my arm around her neck to give her a noogie. "I told you I'm a sergeant. You do not refer to me as sir."

She tries to push me away, but I use my hold on her to sniff her hair. It smells of lavender and springtime despite there being several inches of snow on the ground outside. I wonder how the rest of her skin smells. My pants tighten at those thoughts, and I allow her to push me away before the situation becomes obvious.

As soon as she's free, she escapes to the other side of the kitchen island to gather plates and silverware. I decide to begin the getting to know each other portion of the evening.

"I grew up in Michigan," I tell her. "My parents were madly in love. It drove me crazy my entire childhood." It also set the bar incredibly high for any relationship I had. A bar no man or woman has been able to meet until Lexi came into my life.

"How did they respond when you came out as bi-sexual?"

I freeze at her question. I know she has a problem with me being bi-sexual. She hasn't exactly made a secret of it. I don't know exactly what her problem is, but tonight isn't the night to tackle her resistance. First, I'm going to attach myself to her. Afterwards, I'll deal with her reservations about my sexuality.

I force a chuckle. "My mom said she already knew."

"You're close to your mom?"

"I was. She and my dad died in a car crash over ten years ago."

She gasps and rushes to me to throw her arms around me. "I'm sorry."

She squeezes me, and I don't hesitate to wrap my arms around her and haul her near. Having Lexi in my arms is worth the pain the memory of losing my parents brings up. She melts into me, and any doubts I had about making her mine disappear. This woman is mine. She just doesn't know it yet.

"My family drives me absolutely cray cray, but I wouldn't know what to do if I lost my parents."

I jump on the opening she's given me. "Your family – parents and siblings – are all alive?"

I know she's from West Virginia – although she doesn't talk like anyone I've ever met from West Virginia – but I don't know anything else about her family except they're apparently moonshiners. And here I thought moonshiners were a thing of the past.

"My parents are very much alive."

She tilts her head back to gaze up at me. Her lips tip up before she freezes. Shit. She must realize she's cradled in my arms. Before I have a chance to stop her, she shoves away from me. I don't protest. I know it's going to take time to break down the walls Lexi has built. First, I need to find out why she built those walls, to begin with.

"No brothers or sisters?" I ask as I follow her to the living room where she sets the plates down on the coffee table.

"Nope. Thank goodness."

I open the pizza box and place a slice on her plate before handing it to her. "Thank goodness?"

She stills for a moment before throwing me a saucy wink. "A sibling would never have lived up to my greatness. Poor thing."

She's obviously lying but before I can call her on it, she bites into her pizza and moans. It's the same sound she made when I pressed her against the wall and kissed her on New Year's Eve. I can't wait to hear the sound when I've got her laid out in bed before me.

I clear my throat before speaking. "I thought mushrooms on your pizza was wrong?"

She finishes chewing before responding. "And I thought you were smarter."

I chuckle before picking up my own slice of pizza.

Her phone rings and fear flares in her eyes before irritation replaces it. "Are you going to answer it?"

She frowns before wiping the expression from her face. "Nah. It's rude to answer the phone when a *friend* is over."

Silly woman. Thinking emphasizing the word friend is a turn-off for me. The best couples are friends first.

Her phone buzzes with a message, and this time she doesn't bother to hide her irritation. I stand. "Where's your phone?"

I don't wait for her response before stalking to the side table near the door where I remember seeing her phone earlier. I glance at it when I pick it up and notice she has thirty-four messages and twenty missed calls. What the hell is going on here?

I toss the phone in her lap. "Someone's trying awful hard to get in touch with you."

I pretend to return my attention to my pizza, but I don't miss the frustration on her face. "They can keep trying," she mutters.

I know she didn't intend for me to hear what she said, but I'm not letting this woman be in danger. I'm about done with the people I care about being in danger. The trouble began with Hailey having a stalker and hasn't let up since. The most recent example being Val targeted by a client at the law firm she works at.

My protector mode is now firmly engaged. I will keep this woman safe even if I have to fight her the entire time.

"Who's they?"

She startles and fumbles her phone. When she has a hold on it again, she switches it off. "No one important."

"Is it your previous employer?"

Lexi worked together with Chrissie at the CIA. I know Lexi was an analyst who mostly sat behind a desk, but she dealt with terrorists and all kinds of evil men all the same. If one of them is after her now, I'm wading in and keeping her safe.

"Nope," she says and stuffs half the slice of pizza in her mouth.

I cock an eyebrow. Does she seriously think I'm going to accept her non-answer?

She doesn't respond as she takes her sweet time chewing. After she finally swallows, she stares straight into my eyes and says, "My previous employer is not trying to reach me."

She appears sincere but appearances can be deceiving. She was taught by the best in the business to lie after all.

"All right," I say as if I'm going to let this go. I'm lying. I'll talk to Wally and ask him if he can dig anything up. Unlike the rest of us, Wally didn't get out of government service when he retired from the Army. He's got connections I can only dream of.

Lexi picks up the remote control and switches on the television. "What movie do you want to watch?"

"Your choice."

Her smile stretches from ear to ear. "Good 'cuz I'm in the mood to watch someone blow shit up."

I motion to the television. "Have at it."

She finds the latest action and adventure movie and throws the remote on the coffee table before curling into the opposite corner of the sofa. Not happening. She's entirely too far away from me. I glide closer and wrap my arm around her shoulders. I use my hold on her shoulders to draw her near until she's cuddled into my side.

"Friends don't cuddle on the sofa together," she protests, but she doesn't try to pull away from me. Which is a good thing since I'm on high alert after seeing the number of messages and calls on her phone.

While Lexi watches the movie, my mind flips through various scenarios. Is Lexi in danger? Does she have a stalker? Not if I can help it. I squeeze her shoulders. Not if I can help it.

Chapter 5

Only the best friendships are built on
a solid foundation of alcohol, sarcasm,
inappropriateness, and shenanigans.

I slow as I walk down the hallway toward the offices of *You Cheat, We Eat.* I don't know if I made the right decision accepting the position of office manager. I'm not worried if I can do the job. The job is a piece of cake. Maybe a little boring, but nothing I can't handle. No, I'm worried I made the decision in haste.

After Lenny came over for pizza last week and 'accidentally' saw the number of messages on my phone, I panicked and decided to stay in Wisconsin for a bit longer. I'm not ready to confront the situation back home yet. Snort. Yet? I never want to deal with the situation. Not in a million lifetimes.

I take a deep breath and straighten my back before unlocking the office door with the key Chrissie gave me. I'm the first to arrive. Chrissie offered to come in and help me get settled, but I declined her offer. I don't need her help.

I'm alone for the first thirty minutes. I use the time to acquaint myself with the offices and the computer software. I'm finishing brewing my second cup of coffee when Hailey strolls in.

"Yes, thank you," she says and steals my coffee right out of my hands.

"I didn't know you enjoy drinking kopi luwak."

Her hand freezes on the way to her mouth. "What's kopi luwak?"

I gesture to the coffee cup in her hand. "What you're drinking." I pause before explaining. "Coffee beans made out of cat crap."

She gags before handing the cup back to me. "Enjoy your coffee."

I down a large gulp and sigh. "It's good. So, so good."

Phoebe and Ryker stroll inside. Ryker makes a beeline for the coffee maker, but Hailey stops him. "I wouldn't if I were you." He cocks an eyebrow at her but doesn't speak. "Our new office manager is using cat poop to make coffee."

Ryker removes the lid from the coffee bean grinder and sniffs. "These aren't kopi luwak beans."

Hailey fists her hands on her hips. "I can't believe you."

"Seriously? You tried to steal my coffee."

Phoebe moans. "Please, stop talking about coffee. This one." She points to her husband. "Won't let me have any caffeine despite the doctor saying I could have one cup a day."

"Not taking any chances."

"And I love you for wanting to take care of me and protect me, but I need a cup of coffee, for crying out loud!" Her voice rises until she's shrieking at the end of her statement.

I hand her my cup. "Here. You can have a sip of mine."

She inhales the scent while I place myself in front of her husband who looks ready to filet me. "One sip isn't going to hurt her or the baby."

His response? A grunt.

"We need to work on your manners."

Another grunt.

I ignore him and retrieve my coffee cup from Phoebe before she can inhale the entire cup in one go. Moving on. "Where are the dogs?" I ask Hailey.

"Aiden's bringing them later. He's on swing shift today."

Aiden is her husband. He's also a police detective. They know each other from high school but didn't get together until recently. Good choice. Marrying young is not the way to go. Trust me. I know.

"Do you have any instructions for me this morning?" I ask.

"Um…"

While Hailey tries to come up with a response, Ryker and Phoebe settle in their office. From what Chrissie told me, Ryker's usually out of the office hunting fugitives but now that his wife is pregnant, he's not leaving her alone. As in he comes to the office with her every day whether he has work to do or not.

I settle behind Chrissie's desk. No, my desk. "I'll go through the emails while you figure it out," I tell Hailey.

"Sounds good," she says and escapes into her office.

I spend the next hour responding to emails. I also do a few background checks for Hailey and Phoebe. Based on what I've seen, Hailey works mostly on catching cheating spouses in the act while Phoebe handles insurance claim investigations.

I notice a woman on the camera feed and stand to greet her when she opens the door.

"Hi, welcome to—"

"Where's my husband?" she screams.

I don't tell her to calm down. The worst thing you can do in this situation is tell a woman to calm down.

"Who's your husband?"

She stomps toward me. "You know who he is."

I bite my lip and adopt my 'I have no idea what's going on' face. "I'm sorry. Today's my first day. I'm not caught up on all the case files yet."

"My husband is Chet Rawlings. Where is he?"

I hear Hailey approach from behind me, and I shake my head slightly. She must notice the movement as she freezes. I hear the snick of the lock on the other office door and know Phoebe's protected. Good. I can concentrate on Mrs. Crazy now.

I sit behind my desk and wiggle my mouse to wake my screen. "Which investigator handled your file?"

"How the hell would I know?"

Alrighty then. Ms. Crazy is not going to be helpful. Good to know.

"Did you hire Hailey McGraw?"

"I didn't hire anyone," she shrieks. Note to self: buy earplugs for in the office.

Okay, if she didn't hire anyone, it means her husband was either being investigated for insurance fraud or he's a fugitive Ryker picked up.

"When was the last time you saw your husband?"

"When someone from this office cuffed him and dragged him away!" Fugitive it is.

She draws a handgun from her bag and waves it around. I barely contain my eyeroll. Does she expect me to be intimidated by a gun? I can see from here the safety's on. It's probably not even loaded.

I sigh before standing and rounding my desk to approach the woman. Before she can blink, I reach forward and snatch the weapon out of her hand. I throw it on my desk before seizing her arm and wrenching it behind her back.

"Ryker! Cuffs!"

Ryker appears with a pair of flex cuffs, and I secure her hands behind her back before dumping her into a chair.

"Call Aiden."

Hailey enters the room and wiggles her phone at me. "Already done."

Phoebe peeks around her door. "Can I come out now?"

I nod, but Ryker growls and moves to stand in front of her. Phoebe is in her second trimester. It's going to be a long three plus months with him doing his caveman act whenever anyone's around his pregnant wife.

Hailey's staring at me with her mouth hanging open. "What? Do I have something on my face?"

I rub a hand over my mouth, but I don't feel anything.

"Wow. You're even better than Chrissie."

I smirk. "Can you repeat that so I can record it and send it to her?"

Her brow wrinkles. "I thought you two were friends."

"Well, yeah. Only the best of friends compete with each other." I wink.

"Hello!" The woman screeches. "You handcuffed me to a chair! What gives you the right to mishandle me?"

This time I don't bother holding in my eyeroll. "What gives you the right to wave a gun in my face?" Oh, yeah. The gun. I pick it up from my desk and field strip it. "Do we have evidence bags?"

Hailey's mouth is gaping open again. "I thought you were an analyst."

I frown. Why does everyone assume analysts don't know how to do diddly-squat? We get the same initial training as everyone else. I blame the movies. They always make analysts out to be geeks who don't know the barrel from the butt of a weapon. I'm no geek, and I definitely know the ins and outs of more weapons than I'd ever know what to do with.

"You're violating my civil rights." Mrs. Crazy can't stop herself, can she?

Before I can give her a lesson on what civil rights are and why I'm not violating hers, Aiden rushes into the office with his weapon raised. At the rate I'm going, my eyes are going to get stuck in the back of my head from all the eye-rolling while I'm working here.

"Good grief, Aiden." Hailey huffs. "What's with the full-on SWAT reaction? Everyone here has been thoroughly trained on weapons and how to disarm an assailant."

He holsters his weapon before approaching her. "You can never be too careful." He kisses her hair before assessing the situation.

"What did she do?" he asks Hailey, but the woman answers.

"I didn't do nothing. She attacked me." She nods toward me.

"Did you attack her?" Aiden asks.

I roll my eyes. "She waved a gun in my face. I disarmed her and secured her until you arrived."

Hailey bounces on her toes. "It was awesome!"

My phone rings reminding me why I'm not awesome. As if I needed the reminder. I should get a new phone number but changing my number would probably make matters worse. I force those thoughts out of my mind and concentrate on what's going on in the room.

Too bad ignoring the problem won't cause it to disappear.

Chapter 6

"Evening everybody!" I shout when I enter McGraw's Pub.

"Hey, Lexi," is shouted in return by Lenny and his friends from their table in the corner where they're playing poker. What a shocker.

Lenny and his former military buddies – aka Wally, Barney, Sid, and Max – practically live at McGraw's. Max, who owns the pub, left the military early when Hailey was born. When the rest of them retired, they decided Milwaukee was as good a place as any to land. They helped to raise Hailey after her mom took off, and now she calls all of them her 'uncles'.

I'm probably giving away my age by saying this but walking into McGraw's Pub makes me feel like I'm on an episode of *Cheers*. Everybody certainly knows my name here. Although I haven't been in Milwaukee long, Chrissie and her friends have embraced me into their group.

I've missed being part of a group. Working at Langley didn't exactly lend itself to close friendships. Keeping secrets all the time isn't the best way to make friends.

"Hey, Lexi." Barney motions me over. "Why did the fan blow itself?" Barney is *that* friend. The one who takes inappropriate to a new level.

"Because it was turned on!" He guffaws before raising a hand. I slap it.

There's no sense berating the man. He's going to do his thing no matter what. And Barney's thing is telling dirty jokes. I'd say I don't know how his girlfriend, Val, puts up with it, but she's nearly as bad as him with telling inappropriate jokes. It's a match made in heaven. If heaven were a place with dirty old men and outrageous women who lack brain-to-mouth filters.

"Hey, Whiskey," Lenny says as he stands and kisses my hair. My body automatically sways toward him, but I manage to stop myself before I melt into him like some romance novel heroine. *Gag.*

"He called her whiskey! I'm totally winning this bet," Phoebe announces from behind me.

I pat her arm. "Silly girl. No one's winning the bet."

She raises an eyebrow in challenge before asking Lenny, "Did you hear about how Lexi took on an armed woman at the office today?" She looks at me and pretends to drop a microphone. Oh, ye of little faith. If she thinks switching on Lenny's overprotectiveness is the way to my heart, she doesn't know me at all.

Lenny growls, and I roll my eyes as if the sound doesn't cause tingles to erupt over my body. Wait. Wait. Wait. It doesn't. There is no tingling happening here. None at all. And my pants didn't burst into flames when I lied. Nope.

"What the hell happened?"

He needs to stop using his growly voice before I decide to say screw it and find out how quickly he can make me a happy camper. Abort. Abort. I need to get out of here. I whirl around, intent on making my escape, but Lenny captures my hand to stop me.

"What happened? Are you in danger?"

"What is it with you men and jumping to conclusions?" Val scoffs at Lenny before sitting down next to her boyfriend, Barney. When he smiles at her, his eyes light up.

"You were in danger, Trouble."

Barney will never admit it, but Val having some client from the law firm where she works after her was to his benefit. He took the opportunity to move her into his apartment and she never left. Not even after the bad guy was caught and jailed. In fact, the two recently bought a house and got a dog.

I decide it's time to make things loud and clear to Lenny.

"I am not in danger."

"But the—"

I hold up my hand to stop him. "Repeat after me. Lexi is not in danger."

Suzie claps behind me. "Are we getting to the portion of the evening where Lexi spills her secrets?"

"We are not," I tell her.

"Baby Rossi's hungry." Phoebe rubs her belly. "Can we eat now and pry secrets out of Lexi later?"

I use the opportunity to pull myself away from Lenny and thread my arm through Phoebe's. We march to a table where Hailey, Suzie, and Chrissie join us.

"Where's Faith?"

"She's helping my step-brother with a homework assign-ment," Hailey answers.

Faith was a single mother when she met Hailey's dad, Max. When Max proposed, her son, Oliver, asked Max to adopt him. He didn't hesitate to say yes, which is why Max and Faith married in secret before their actual Valentine's Day wedding.

"On a Friday night?"

"Someone got in trouble for fighting this week."

Poor Ollie. Faith is an advocate for non-violence. Unfortunately, Max and his military brothers don't agree with her outlook and taught Ollie how to fight.

"Someone's sleeping on the sofa tonight," I sing as Max approaches us. Judging by the smirk on his face, he's confident he'll convince Faith to let him sleep in bed with her tonight.

"Hey, Pops." Hailey gets to her feet to hug her dad.

"Hey, Babycakes. What can I get everyone?"

"We need a bottle of tequila."

At Hailey's words, I snicker. "You gonna try to drink me under the table?"

"Not me. Chrissie is."

Chrissie grins. "No. I thought we'd play pool instead."

I shrug. "I'm happy to play pool with you, but I already told you there's nothing to know about Lenny and me."

"Except he calls you whiskey!" Suzie yells loud enough for the entire bar to hear. Sure enough, when I glance over my shoulder, Lenny is staring at me. Awesome. Freaking awesome.

"He can call me whatever name he wants. It doesn't mean we're together."

Suzie points to him. "But have you seen the man? Don't you want to ride his disco stick?"

I tap my cheek as if I'm considering the question. "I don't know. Does it have strobe lights?"

Chrissie elbows Suzie. "Enough. Tonight isn't about Lenny and Lexi." She stares at me. "It's about why Lexi quit the job she loves and is hiding out in Milwaukee."

Huh. Does she think there's some big secret about me quitting the agency? Rest assured. There isn't. Hiding out in Milwaukee is an entirely different story. One I have no plans on telling her or anyone else. No matter how nosy he is.

"Can we eat first?" Suzie asks right before her tummy rumbles.

The entire time we're eating, Chrissie stares at me as if she's daring me to spill my secrets. Did she forget who she's dealing with? This is going to be fun.

Two hours later I realize my mistake. I may have grown up playing pool, but I haven't played much since. D.C. isn't exactly known for its pool halls, after all. Chrissie, on the other hand, has been playing pool with all sorts of shady characters in dive bars all over the world.

"Ready to give up yet?" Chrissie asks as she chalks her cue for another round.

"I will never surrender!" I throw a fist in the air in case my words leave any doubt.

Hailey arrives with a tray of tequila shots. I grab one before raising an eyebrow in challenge at Chrissie. The woman can hold her liquor better than most but not as good as me, and she knows it. She also can't refuse a challenge. She sighs but lifts her glass in the air.

"No retreat! No surrender!" I salute before downing my shot.

We play another game, and I manage to win this one by the skin of my teeth. While Hailey racks for our next round, I survey the remaining patrons in the pub. Phoebe is long gone, and Suzie is curled up in a booth asleep.

"Where's Grayson?" Surely, her husband isn't happy with his pregnant wife hanging out in a bar all night. The question is barely out of my mouth before he arrives. He doesn't say a word as he picks up his wife and carries her to the door.

"She's going to be pissed she missed hearing your big secret," Hailey says. Or I think she says. Her words are getting a bit hard to decipher at this point.

"Last call!" Max shouts.

Last call? It can't be closing time yet. But when I do another sweep of the pub, I notice the only people left in the bar are Hailey, Chrissie, and me as well as Wally and Lenny. Barney dragged Val home a while ago, and Sid took off when Mary Ann messaged she was on break at the hospital.

Chrissie returns the pool cue to its spot on the wall. "Time's up. Why did you quit your job?"

I can't help the smile forming on my face. "You're going to be mighty disappointed when you hear."

Hailey groans. "Don't tell me it's something stupid like you got caught boinking a co-worker in the restrooms."

"First of all, no one uses the word boink anymore. Second, the restroom? Ew. And last, but not least, you don't have sex with a co-worker unless you're asking for trouble."

Chrissie pales at my words. "Dang it." I grab her hands and squeeze. "I didn't mean—" I blow out a breath. "I'm an idiot."

Hailey's gaze ping-pongs between the two of us. There's a spark of curiosity in her eyes. Before she can ask any questions – questions Chrissie will refuse to answer but will inflame Hailey's curiosity – I tell them what they've been waiting to hear.

"I quit because of how they treated you. The way they threw away a loyal employee over one stupid mistake?" It wasn't one stupid mistake. It was one colossal mistake, but I'm not talking about it in front of Hailey.

Chrissie squeezes my hands in response. She doesn't need to say anything. I understand. She's thanking me for my loyalty to her. She's always had my loyalty. From the end of the first day of training when she lied to one of the trainers about the moonshine I'd smuggled in belonging to her, she's had my loyalty. And I've had hers.

Wally throws his arm around her shoulders. "You ready to go home now, Angel?" She nods and he kisses her hair. "Come on, kid." He gives Hailey a chin lift. "We'll give you a ride."

As Hailey trails after the couple, Lenny sidles up to me. "I'm taking you home."

"I don't need a ride. I'm perfectly sober."

He frowns. "You may appear sober but based on all you had to drink this evening, you'll blow above the legal limit."

Crap on a cracker. He's right. "Fine." I huff. "But no hanky-panky."

"No hanky-panky."

He agreed way too easily. Maybe I've had more to drink than I thought. I motion to the door. "Lead away, dear fellow. Lead away."

He places a hand on my lower back and guides me to the exit. Even through the gazillion layers of clothing necessary to survive a Wisconsin winter, I can feel the heat of his hand. I wish it were on my skin.

I force those thoughts right out of my mind. No thinking about sexy times with a man who sees entirely too much.

Chapter 7

I'll show you mine, if you'll show me yours ~
words no friend should ever utter.

LENNY

Excitement pulses in my veins as I drive Lexi home. I know this means nothing to her. She's only letting me drive her home because she doesn't want a DUI, but she doesn't get it. Trusting me to get her home safe means something to me. Trusting me with her safety period means the world to me.

I pull into the driveway and switch off the engine to my SUV.

"Wait there," I tell Lexi when I notice her reach for the handle.

She stares straight into my eyes as she clutches the handle and pushes the door open. Little shit. I jump out and rush around to meet her. She sways as she shuts the door behind her. I steady her with a hand on her lower back.

"Come on. Let's get you to bed."

"There will be no taking Lexi to bed. Lexi will take herself to bed!" She punches her fist into the air with her pronouncement.

I chuckle. "Exactly how much have you had to drink tonight?"

She shrugs. "Hailey sure loves her tequila shots."

I lead her to the front door. When she removes her key from her purse, I snatch it from her and use it to open the door. As soon as we enter, the alarm beeps. I walk to the panel.

"Did you change the code from when Wally lived here?"

Her eyebrows fly to the top of her head. "You know Wally's security code? What about Wally being a super-secret spy?"

She's yanking my chain. She knows as well as I do exactly what kind of black ops work Wally did. The woman has a security clearance higher than mine after all. Had. She's no longer working for the agency.

I know this for certain since I asked Wally to ascertain whether Lexi was in danger from her job at the agency. He assured me she's no longer an employee, and there is no talk of her being in danger.

Lexi bumps me out of the way. "It's not my first day on the job. Obviously, I changed the security code."

After she punches in the numbers, she turns around and points to the door. "You may leave now."

I stalk toward her. "I'm not leaving."

Her eyes narrow. "You promised no hanky-panky."

I smirk. "Define hanky-panky."

If looks could kill, I'd be stone cold dead with the lasers her eyes are shooting at me right now. And I must be some kind of sick bastard because my pants tighten. Her passion – even when it's her being mad at me – is one big turn on for me.

She throws her hands in the air. "I knew I couldn't trust you."

Her words are the equivalent of a bucket of ice water being thrown on my libido. I shackle her wrists. "You can trust me, Whiskey."

She squirms in my hold. "I can't trust you," she seethes. "You promised no hanky-panky and you're going back on your promise."

Her gaze dips to below my waist, and I know exactly what she's planning. Before she has a chance to knee me in the groin, I yank her close. "And I intend to fulfill my promise. All I wanted to know is if a kiss falls under hanky-panky?"

Her breaths increase until she's panting. I can feel her breasts rubbing against me as she gasps for breath. She doesn't give in, though. Not my Lexi. "Do we need to have the discussion about friend zone again?"

I dip my head to glide my nose along her neck. Goosebumps break out along her skin. Her response to me is why I won't give up. I know she wants me, but she doesn't want to want me. The question is why.

As if prompted by my internal musings, her telephone rings. I step away from her to nab her purse from where she threw it on the chair near the door. I thrust it into her hands.

"Answer it," I demand.

She rolls her eyes before removing her phone from her purse. She stares straight into my eyes while she switches off her phone.

"Damn it, woman. What is going on?"

She gets all up in my face. "What's going on is none of your doggone business, friend," she snarls before stomping to the door and flinging it open. "Thank you for the ride home. Your services are no longer required."

I march to the door and slam it shut. "If you think I'm leaving, you've lost your damn mind."

She presses up on her tiptoes and gets in my face. "Don't make me call Wally on you."

I chuckle. "Go ahead."

She powers up the phone still in her hand and punches in Chrissie's number. I snatch the phone from her before it can connect and end the call.

She crosses her arms over her chest and leans against the door. "I thought you didn't care if I called Wally."

I should have known better than to call Lexi's bluff. She doesn't back down from a dare. The woman spent six hours playing pool tonight rather than give in and tell her best friend why she quit her job after all. It's possible I've underestimated her level of stubbornness.

"I don't think Wally and Chrissie will appreciate you interrupting them at the moment."

She giggles. "It won't be the first time."

I need to consider another approach with her. Bulldozing Lexi is getting me nowhere. And I have the perfect idea.

"Do you want to know why I have such a large SUV?"

I know she does. She's been teasing me about a bachelor owning an SUV with seating for nine people since the first time she saw it.

Her eyes light up, but she quickly blanks her face to hide her interest. She shrugs. "I guess."

"I'll show you why I have the SUV if you have dinner with me tomorrow."

"You should tell me because we're friends. Friends tell each other stuff."

I cock an eyebrow. "The same way you've told me about all those phone calls and messages?"

She flinches, and I want to retract my words. Except, I can't. I need to know who is bothering her. Is the person dangerous? Is she in danger?

"The calls don't matter." She's obviously lying, but I let it slide. I'm not going to win this argument tonight. I concentrate on what I can win instead.

"Do we have a deal? I'll show you why I have the SUV if you have dinner with me tomorrow night."

"Dinner as friends. It's not a date."

I acquiesce despite my intent to ensure the dinner is as romantic as possible. I'll open up to her about my past and hopefully, it will prompt her to open up to me in return.

She sticks out her hand, and we shake on it. Her skin is soft, and I'm tempted to use my hold on her to draw her near, but I know better. She'd kick me in the groin before I have a chance to feel those lush lips on mine again.

We stand there holding hands for several seconds. I don't let go. It's Lexi's move. Her phone beeps with a message and brings her out of her reverie while I swallow my growl. Patience, Lenny. Patience.

She clears her throat and motions to the door. "I'll see you tomorrow."

I stay right where I am. She's not going to be happy about this part, but she did agree. "In order to show you why I have the SUV, we need to get an early start tomorrow. It makes more sense if I sleep here."

She opens her mouth to speak – probably to yell at me for tricking her – and a vein in her forehead pulses as she glares at me. I shrug as if I didn't intentionally mislead her.

"Whatever," she finally says. "I'm going to bed."

She stomps past me, but I snatch her hand to stop her. "Good night, Whiskey." I kiss her forehead and let my lips linger on her skin. Skin I have every intention of tasting every single inch of. Her breath catches and her eyes dilate before she sways toward me.

"Sweet dreams."

She clears her throat. "Yeah, yeah. Sleep well."

She marches to the hallway and a second later I hear her bedroom door slam shut.

I settle into the sofa and switch on the television. With the object of my every desire sleeping mere feet away, there will be no sleep for me. It'll be worth it in the end, though. I need to be patient is all.

Chapter 8

If you want a stable friendship, get a horse.

I'M ALREADY AWAKE WHEN Lenny knocks on my bedroom door the next morning. Despite the large amount of alcohol I consumed last night, I didn't get much sleep. How could I when the man who makes me want to forget all about why we shouldn't be together slept mere feet from me?

"I'm up," I shout at the door.

"We need to leave in thirty minutes."

I roll out of bed and get to my feet. "Got it!"

I shower as fast as I can and put on jeans and a sweater. I have no idea what Lenny's going to show me today, but I assume comfortable clothing is the way to go.

When I open my bedroom door, the smell of bacon wafts my way. My stomach rumbles in response. I enter the kitchen to discover Lenny making breakfast without a shirt on. My breath hitches when the expanse of muscles on his back comes into view. Men in their fifties aren't supposed to resemble a wet dream.

My gaze travels down, and I notice he's not wearing shoes or socks. Curse him. I love a man in jeans with bare feet. It probably shows off my hillbilly roots, but I could care less as I stand here studying the object of my fantasies.

"You going to stand there staring at me all day or are you going to come in here and eat some breakfast?"

Busted. "I wasn't drooling over you. I was wondering how stupid it is to work with bacon fat in bare skin."

Just in case, I swipe at my mouth to check there's no drool showing before moving past Lenny to open the cabinet with the plates in it.

"Whiskey, you can drool over me all you want."

Crap. Did I say drool out loud? I did. Such an idiot. Time to nip this in the bud. "Let's eat. Aren't you the one who said we needed to leave early for you to show me your big secret?"

We settle on the breakfast bar with plates of bacon and eggs. It smells delicious and I don't hesitate to dig in. When I realize Lenny's staring at me, I pause with a piece of bacon hanging in the air.

"What? A girl's gotta eat."

He shrugs. "I didn't expect you to be able to eat after the amount you drank last night."

"You, my friend, don't know me as well as you think you do."

He leans forward. "But I want to get to know you better," he rasps out.

Ugh! What is wrong with me? I swear I don't say things to challenge him on purpose. Really, I don't.

I keep my mouth shut while we finish eating. Correction – not shut-shut. I can't eat through osmosis, but I don't speak again until we're loaded up in his SUV.

"Where are we going?"

"You'll see."

"If you going to try something kinky, I'll have you know I've got moves."

"We'll figure out a safe word." He winks over at me.

"I have a safe word all right. It's 'friend zone'. Learn it. Live by it."

He chuckles as he backs out of the driveway and heads downtown. Except we don't go downtown. We travel Northwest of downtown to Sherman Park instead. He comes to a halt in front of a low-rise apartment building, which has seen better days and honks the horn.

The door flies open, and a kid runs out. He doesn't hesitate to open the back door of the SUV and hop in.

"Hey, old man. How's it hanging?"

When Lenny glances back at the kid, the happiness is practically pouring from him. He's super excited to see this kid. Is it his kid? The plot thickens.

"Hey, Darren. This is Lexi."

Darren leans forward in his seat to get a good look at me. "Is Lexi your girlfriend? Lenny and Lexi sitting in a tree. K-I-S-S-I-N-G."

I giggle. "Kids still sing that?"

The singing stops. "Who are you calling a kid? I'm fourteen."

I raise my hands in surrender. "Oops. My bad."

"Geez. You must be as old as the old man. No one says my bad anymore."

"How old do you think I am?"

He scrunches up his nose as he studies me. "Old. Real old. At least Forty."

Forty is old? Dang. I must be ancient at forty-nine. I'm not giving him any additional fuel for the fire by telling him my exact age, though. I know better.

"Sounds about right," I say instead.

He punches a fist in the air. "Called it!"

Lenny stops in front of a two-story townhouse. The paint is chipped off and the porch seems ready to collapse at any moment. He hits the horn, and another kid rushes out the door. He jumps over the stairs and rushes to the door.

He fist bumps Darren before settling into his seat.

"The old man has a girlfriend," Darren tells the kid. "And she's old."

The kid peers through the front seats to study me. "She's a MILF. I'd do her."

I giggle, but Lenny is not amused. "Don't be disrespectful."

"How is it disrespectful to tell a woman she's doable?"

"Son, trust me. It is."

"Who's your friend, Darren?" I ask before the kid has a chance to respond.

"I'm Brandon. You can call me Bran."

We continue driving through the various neighborhoods of Milwaukee until the SUV is packed full of teenage boys. Before I can gag on the smell of wet socks and sweat, Lenny parks in the lot of an ice arena.

The doors of the SUV fly open, and the kids jump out. They race toward the entrance not worried one bit about the icy, slippery parking lot. I start to follow them, but then I notice Lenny at the rear of his vehicle.

"What's all this?" I ask as he drags out two large duffle bags before slamming the door shut.

"Hockey gear."

I reach over to grab one of the bags, but he nudges my hand away. "I got it."

"Stubborn," I mumble.

He throws an arm around my shoulder. "Pot, meet kettle."

I elbow him. "I'm not stubborn."

He chuckles as he opens the door to the ice arena. The kids are busy putting on their skates when we join them. Where did those come from? None of the kids had so much as a bag with him.

Lenny points to the skate rental. "The ice arena donates skate rentals to the kids."

"Are you their coach?"

"Coach, mentor, teenage wrangler."

Darn it. He's got a big heart stashed below those muscles? Great. It's going to be even more difficult to resist him now.

He whistles when we reach the ice rink. "Warm up time!"

The boys moan and groan, but not one of them dares to talk back to Lenny as they head out onto the ice and begin skating in circles.

I watch as Lenny unloads the gear. I notice it's well-worn and doesn't match, but there's enough for all six kids. Once he's finished, he grasps my hand and tugs me away from the ice.

"You don't have to stay. I can call a car for you."

"Are you kidding? I'm staying." I wouldn't miss this for the world. "What can I do to help?"

He rewards me with a smile. "You don't mind helping?"

I roll my eyes. "I'm not some wilting flower. I can help."

He motions to a bag of water bottles. "Can you fill these up?"

"No problem."

Before I can nab the bag, he draws me near, and his lips land on mine. I should probably protest, but the second his lips touch mine, I lose my mind. I thread my hands through his hair and draw him near. Lenny groans in return before forcing his tongue past my lips to explore my mouth.

Whistles, catcalls, and cheers erupt behind us. I drag myself away from Lenny and glance over my shoulder to find the kids standing at the entrance to the ice. None of them is bothering to hide their interest in what Lenny and I are doing.

"Told you she's his girlfriend," Darren announces to the group.

"I'm not his girlfriend," I say despite knowing better than to engage with a bunch of kids.

"They must be friends with benefits," Brandon says. "I get it. My mom has lots of friends with benefits."

My eyes widen, and Lenny frowns at Brandon's announcement. He obviously decides not to tackle the issue when he yells, "I thought you guys were here to play hockey. Instead, you're standing around gossiping like a bunch of fishwives."

"Fishwives? What's a fishwife?"

"Dude, obviously it's a woman who looks like a fish."

"No, I think it's a woman who's married to a sailor."

"Whatever. Race you." Darren skates off and the rest of the group follows him.

I groan. "You couldn't volunteer with girl scouts?"

"What in the world am I going to teach a bunch of girls?"

I glare at him. "I'll be sure to mention your comment to Hailey on Monday morning."

He palms my neck and uses his hold to bring me close. "Maybe I should call you trouble instead of whiskey."

"Maybe you should pay attention to the kids you're supposed to be mentoring before they tear the ice arena down."

I point to where the group is jumping from the ice over the boards into the front row of the stands.

"Crap. I can't take my eye off of them for two seconds." Lenny marches off blowing his whistle.

Phew. I grab the bag of water bottles and go in search of the restrooms. I need to cool down and remind myself Lenny is a friend. Just a friend. I don't date man whores, remember? Plus, there's the other problem. The one I'm ignoring like a champ.

Chapter 9

My friend, Pandora, is ready to take our friendship to the next level, but I'm not ready to open that box.

LENNY

I knock on Lexi's front door before backing away a bit. When she sees what I'm holding in my hands, she's going to be angry, and I want to make certain I'm out of kneeing range. I could disable her before her knee came anywhere near me if I wanted to. The problem is – I don't want to. I want to give her everything she wants. Except keeping me in the friend zone.

She opens the door and frowns when she sees the flowers in my hands. "You don't give flowers to friends."

"Not true. I know for a fact it's normal to give friends flowers in Europe."

She motions toward the bouquet. "I mean red roses. You don't give red roses to friends."

"You're more than a friend to me. I care about you."

Her mouth opens and closes a few times while she tries to come up with a response. I know better than to give her time.

Every moment of time she's allowed to spend thinking, she uses to build her walls and push me away. Not on my watch.

I press past her and make my way to the kitchen. I open and close the cabinets searching for a vase before I realize this is Wally's place. Of course, there's no vase. I find a jug instead and fill it with water. I arrange the flowers and set the jug on the kitchen counter.

When I finish, I find Lexi frowning at me. "What's wrong?" Besides the obvious.

"You're awful comfortable here. Have you and Wally…" Her words drop off, and she bites her lip.

I don't make her wait for a response. I know what she wants to know. I prowl to her and pinch her chin to make certain I have her full attention before answering. "No. Wally and I have never been intimate. I have not been intimate with any of my brothers."

"But you hit on them all the time."

I chuckle. "It's called teasing."

Her mouth drops open in a perfect O and my resistance takes a flying leap out the window. I lean over and place my lips on hers. My hand travels from pinching her chin to cradling her cheek. Her skin is silky smooth. I want to feel her skin against my naked skin, but I know it's too soon. I force myself to end the kiss.

My hand caresses her cheek one more time before I drop it to grasp her hand. "We have reservations."

"Where are we going?" she asks once we're in my vehicle traveling toward downtown.

"It's a surprise."

She crosses her arms over her chest. "One thing to know about me. I don't enjoy surprises."

"Oh?" I glance over at her briefly before returning my gaze to the road in front of us. "You enjoy giving surprises but not getting them?"

She surprised the hell out of Chrissie when she showed up for her wedding on Christmas day.

She shrugs. "Maybe."

I park on the street in front of the restaurant. Her nose scrunches as she stares at the building. I expected this response. The restaurant may serve the best Italian food in the city, but the place has the appearance of a hole in the wall. At least, from the outside it does.

"Wait there," I order.

She rolls her eyes but doesn't move. I open the door for her and help her out. Her skirt creeps up her thighs and I notice a slit up the right side nearly to her hip. My nostrils flare and I plaster her to my side. I don't want any other man getting ideas about this woman.

"I guess you like my skirt."

"It's not the type of skirt you wear for your friends," I tell her as I open the door for her.

She gasps when she sees the interior of the restaurant. It's a typical Italian restaurant design with red checkered tablecloths, candles in Chianti bottles in the middle of the tables, and a red and white checkered floor. The lighting is dim making the ambience romantic.

Lexi whirls on me and grits out, "This is not a date."

I don't have time to respond before the hostess greets us. "Mr. Walker. I have your table ready."

She leads us to a corner from which I can observe the entire restaurant. I pull out a chair for Lexi. She huffs but allows me to help her into her seat.

I smile when I sit across from her. Judging by the vein pulsing in her forehead, she's irritated. I enjoy riling her up. She's adorable when she's mad. Someday soon I'll have the right to kiss her annoyance right off of her face.

The waitress arrives and hands us a pair of menus. "Will you allow me to order for you?" I ask Lexi.

"Go for it. I haven't had a say in anything that's happened this evening yet. Why change things now?"

I ignore her snippy comment and order a family-style platter of spaghetti and meatballs with garlic bread for our main course and stuffed mushrooms for an appetizer. I also order a bottle of red wine for Lexi and a beer for me.

Once the waitress leaves, Lexi leans forward and hisses at me, "Okay, we're here. Tell me."

I don't bother pretending to not know what she's talking about. While I enjoy watching the vein pulse in her forehead, I don't want it to burst open.

"Tell you? I already showed you why I own the SUV today."

"You showed me the what. You didn't tell me the why."

I give myself a few seconds to gather my courage. It's not as if what I'm going to tell her is a secret. My brothers know all about it. And I know if I want to move beyond mere friendship with her, I need to open up. Hopefully, my opening up will lead to her telling me what the hell is going on with the phone calls she refuses to answer.

"I want children," I say.

Her brow wrinkles. "And? You can still have children. A man's ability to have children doesn't have an expiry date on it unlike with women."

"I've never been able to have them."

Her eyes widen, and she reaches across the table to squeeze my hand. "I'm sorry. I didn't realize you're impotent."

"I'm not impotent," I snarl.

She retracts her hand. "I don't understand."

"It's impossible to find a woman who can handle my bisexuality."

It's the reason I initially stayed away from Lexi after all. I know she has an issue with it, but I'm done waiting for her to deal with her issues on her own. We'll work through them together.

"Bullshit."

Bullshit? "What do you mean bullshit?"

"Your bisexuality is not a problem. You just haven't met the right woman yet. A woman who understands being bisexual is not a threat to her."

My breath catches, and I have to remind myself oxygen is necessary to sustain life. I force myself to inhale as my heart races in my chest.

"I thought you had a problem with my sexuality."

Her nose scrunches in that cute way of hers. "What gave you that idea?"

"How about you running away anytime I come near? Forcing me into the friend zone."

"Oh, that."

"Exactly. That."

She shrugs. "I don't care if you're bisexual. Although, a conversation would need to be had. I'm not okay with cheating."

"Then, why am I in the friend zone?" She opens her mouth, but I stop her with a wag of my finger. "And don't you dare tell me you aren't attracted to me."

"Maybe I'm not attracted to you."

"You're lying. I'm not some teenage boy who's never had a woman in his arms. I know when a woman is interested."

"My body may be interested. It doesn't mean I am."

"Explain."

The waitress arrives and sets our appetizers on the table. Lexi snags a mushroom and stuffs it into her mouth. Her face goes red, and she fans her mouth. "Hot. Hot. Hot."

I hand her a glass of water, and she downs the entire thing while swallowing the mushroom.

As soon as she's done coughing, I say, "Nice attempt at avoiding answering the question. I give you a B."

"A B? Burning the roof of my mouth is worth a B+ at the very least."

I drum my fingers on the table and pretend to re-consider my evaluation. "Okay. B+, but now you need to answer the question. No more avoiding."

"I'd think the answer would be obvious."

"Okay, Ms. Avoidance. Care to explain to the rest of the class?"

"You're a man whore."

I freeze. She's teased me about being a man whore before, but I thought she was just joking. "What makes you think I'm a man whore?"

She rolls her eyes. "Please. Everyone knows about you taking three men home at once."

How does she know about that? It was before Christmas – the day Lexi barged into my life – when Wally pranked Barney, Sid, and me with three male dates. After Sid and Barney ran away, I offered to show the men a good time and took them home with me.

Shit. I didn't know Lexi knew about it. But I can't deny what happened. There are too many witnesses. Besides, I don't want to lie to Lexi.

"Does it bother you I sleep with men?"

She leans forward to hiss at me. "No, but it sure as hell bothers me you have orgies."

Crap. Making Lexi mine is going to be more work than I expected.

"What if I told you I haven't slept with another person – male or female – since Christmas?"

She snorts. "Two months without sex for the man whore? Really?"

"I haven't slept with anyone since the moment I saw you. I haven't wanted to."

She chews on another mushroom as she studies me for signs I'm lying. I'm not. The only person I can see now is her. I've been biding my time, getting to know her, before making her mine. Not a single other person – male or female – has called to me the way she does.

"Say I believe you—"

"It's the truth."

"Nuh-uh. No interrupting." I motion for her to continue. "Even if I believe you, it doesn't change a thing."

I wait for her to continue, but she doesn't. I want to ask her what's holding her back if she believes me, but I've pushed her enough for one night. I'll just have to continue what I've been doing for the past month – battering at her walls until they come crashing down.

Chapter 10

An acquaintance asks for a favor, a friend
demands a favor with a smile.

"You want me to what?"

Hailey has lost her doggone mind if she thinks I'm going to do this.

"Do you need me to explain what a honeypot is again?"

I glare at her. "Don't be condescending. I know what a honeypot scheme is. What I don't understand is why you want to use me as the 'honey'."

"I told you. Ryker won't let Phoebe be involved in these sting operations any longer."

"I don't know why not," I grumble. "Phoebe is sexy as all get out despite her baby bump."

The door to Hailey's office flings open, and Phoebe marches in. "Thank you! My husband disagrees."

The husband in question grunts as he comes up behind her and wraps an arm around her shoulders to bring her flush to him. "I never said you weren't sexy. I said I didn't want you doing honey traps anymore."

Phoebe snorts. "I think your exact words were 'no more honey traps', grunt, 'too dangerous', grunt."

Ryker leans forward and whispers into her ear too softly for us to hear. Whatever it is must be good as she melts into him before he whisks her away.

Once they're gone and the door is once again shut, Hailey pounces. "Now, do you understand why I need you to do this?"

"Why don't you do it? I'm too old to trap a man."

Her eyes twinkle at my words, and I realize I messed up somehow. "Good thing the man we're going to trap is in his late fifties."

Crap. "Men in their late fifties want younger women, not some nearly fifty-year-old."

Her eyebrow cocks. "Really? Lenny wants a younger woman and not you?"

Son of a biscuit. I walked right into that. I stand. "Whatever. I'll do it, but you can't blame me when it's a disaster."

She claps her hands. "Yeah! This is going to be fun."

I frown at her. "This is work, remember?"

She shrugs. "Work can be fun."

Which is how I find myself sitting at the bar of a hotel that afternoon. Phoebe loaned me one of her dresses. It's loose in the chest area as she's much more endowed than I am, but, otherwise, it's skintight and incredibly uncomfortable. I can't believe anyone chooses to dress this way.

"Stop squirming," Hailey says from where she stands behind me.

"Are you serious? You're the one who refuses to get dressed up despite this being your job. I was hired as an office manager. Not for whatever you call this. Did you make Chrissie do this?"

"And incur the wrath of Wally the super-secret agent?" She shudders.

I blow out a puff of air. "How many times do I have to explain? It's not super-secret if everyone knows about it."

The bartender coughs and lifts his chin toward the entrance. "Incoming."

Hailey slaps the room key down on the counter. "Remember. I need compromising pictures," she says and rushes off.

Wait a minute. She never said anything about compromising pictures. Before I can manage to scramble out of my seat, a group of men saunter into the bar. Dang. It's showtime.

Time to trap Mr. Shaw who is apparently cheating on his wife. Since Hailey couldn't find evidence of him cheating, she decided to use me as bait tonight. Yippee.

I scan the crowd for my target. I know he's fifty-nine, wears a combover, and has a beer belly. I figure the combover will give him away. No one wears a combover anymore. And, looky looky, I'm right. There's one man trying desperately to hold onto his youth by maintaining the three greasy hairs on his head.

Hailey told me to be coy. What she doesn't know is there isn't a coy bone in my body. I bite my lip while batting my eyelashes at him. I probably look like I have something in my eye since I am not the flirting type unless sarcasm counts.

Mr. Shaw makes a beeline for me. Huh. Maybe I should try this more often. What am I thinking? No men for me until I deal with the situation back home. It can't be ignored forever, although I'm going to try.

Mr. Shaw stands close enough I get a whiff of his cologne. Huh. I didn't know men still wore *Old Spice.*

He leers at me before asking, "Hey baby, why don't you sit on my lap, and we'll talk about the first thing that comes up?"

Hell to the no. I hold up my hand and use it to force him back to give me some space. "Are you kidding me? This is your pick-up line?"

He goes to answer, but I stick my hand in his face. "It was a rhetorical question." I cross my arms over my chest as I study him. His eyes dip to my cleavage. I snap my fingers in his face. "Eyes are up here."

"You're the one sitting in the bar making eyes at men."

Oh no, he didn't. "Sit your ass down. It's lesson time."

He doesn't move, so I pull out the barstool next to me with my foot and point to it. "Sit," I bark. He scrambles to sit. Good. At least he can follow directions.

Where to begin? I tap my chin as I consider the question. There is much to discuss, but him disrespecting women is as good a place as any to begin.

"First of all, you do not disrespect a woman by insinuating she's asking to hear your cheesy lines."

"But you..." He sputters.

"Let me explain this again. The mere fact a woman is sitting in a bar by herself doesn't mean you have the right to ogle her breasts. It's disrespectful and will get you nowhere. Do you understand?"

I wait for him to nod before continuing. "Second, sit on my lap and we'll talk about the first thing that comes up? Are you out of your dang mind? Are you trying to pick up a woman? Or are you trying to get your ass thrown in jail for being a creeper?"

His cheeks flame, but he doesn't respond.

"And? It wasn't a rhetorical question."

"Pick up a woman?" His response comes out sounding more like a question than an answer.

"Which brings us to point number three." I point to his wedding band. "Are you out of your doggone mind? You're married. If you can't be faithful to your wife, talk to her. Maybe get some counseling. But before you stick your dick in another woman, get separated at least. Vows shouldn't be broken."

"I only wanted to flirt a bit," he mumbles.

I snort. "Do you seriously expect me to believe you?"

"My wife complains I'm boring and I don't know how to flirt with her. I thought I'd try flirting with women at the bar. Get my confidence up before asking her out for a nice romantic dinner and flirting with her."

I twirl around on my barstool to motion to Hailey, but she's already standing behind me. "I thought you stayed hidden in the corner."

"Like I thought you'd actually do your job and try to pick up this guy to prove to his wife he's cheating?"

Mr. Shaw's eyes widen. "My wife hired you?"

I point to Hailey. "Technically, she hired Hailey. I'm filling in."

He perks up. "My wife thinks I'm cheating?"

"Yeah, and she hired a PI to prove it so she can divorce your ass. I don't know what you're happy about here."

"She's jealous. There's hope for us yet." He hops down from his barstool, but I clasp his hand to stop him.

"We're not done here."

"I'm not going to sleep with you. I never was." He pauses. "I mean you're pretty and all, but you're not really my type."

I'm going to accept his words as a compliment and move on. "Yes, I understand. I meant this." I wave toward his 'hairstyle'.

He stares at me with a blank expression on his face.

"She means you need to lose the combover," Hailey explains.

"It's true." I agree. "It's not doing you any favors."

He pats his hair. "But—"

"No," I interrupt. "A thousand times no. You aren't fooling anyone. Besides, bald men can be hot."

He perks up. "They can?"

"Sure. Women love to rub their hands over a bald man's head." I don't know where this crap is coming from, but I go with it.

"This is what you're going to do. You're going to run as fast as you can to the nearest barbershop and deal with," I indicate his combover with a twirl of my finger. "Afterwards, you're going to pick up some flowers for your wife and go home."

"What about?" He waves his hand toward Hailey who has a camera wrapped around her neck.

"The answer is tell her the truth. It will always be tell the truth."

He nods before rushing out of the bar. "You're welcome," I call after him.

"Remind me never to ask you to help out with a honeypot again," Hailey mumbles as she collapses onto his barstool.

I smile. My mission here is accomplished.

Chapter 11

Friends tease each other. Best friends prank each other.

LENNY

There's a spring in my step as I enter McGraw's Pub and it's not merely because today is St. Patrick's Day. Although St. Patrick's Day is always a fun day, I'm excited because I know Lexi can't avoid me tonight the way she's been doing since our date – and, make no mistake about it, it was a date – at the Italian place. Time to work on tearing those walls of hers down. I can't wait.

Sid cheers when he sees me. "Mr. My Woman Is Avoiding Me has arrived."

I smirk. "At least my teeth aren't green. Way to go all out on St. Paddy's Day."

He scrubs at his mouth. "Fucker. I thought I got all the green off. I'm about done with people sneaking into my house and messing with my toothpaste. What did I do to you?"

I shrug not bothering to deny it was me who snuck into his house at o'dark thirty this morning. "The lock on your bedroom window is broken by the way."

Sid glares at me. "I'm going to stop brushing my teeth if people don't stop screwing around with my toothpaste."

"And let all your teeth fall out? Way to teach us."

"I bet Mary Ann would love a man without teeth," Max adds.

Barney and Val wander over to the bar to join us. "What's up with the green teeth?" Barney asks.

Sid snarls at him. "I'm getting a new security system," he mutters before picking up his beer and draining it. He's cute. As if there's a security system I can't get around.

Barney's phone rings and he glares down at it. I bite my tongue to stop the grin from forming on my face and giving me away.

"What?" he barks when he answers. "I told you. I didn't buy a timeshare in Limerick." "I didn't make a down payment." "I don't care what your records say." "What bank account?"

Barney's eyes meet mine, and I stare straight back at him with a blank expression on my face. His gaze roves to his wife who isn't attempting to mask her giggles. "Wasn't me," she manages to utter.

Max lifts his hands in surrender while Sid retreats. Barney places a hand over the receiver to ask, "Where's Wally?"

"Right here," Wally says from behind him where he's standing with his arm wrapped around Chrissie. "What's up?"

"Did you sign me up for a timeshare in Ireland?"

Wally chuckles. "Nope."

Barney points at me. "I will get you back," he utters before marching off while trying to explain to the salesperson how he didn't make any deposit.

Val rushes after him. "Hey! Maybe I want to visit Ireland."

"I have fifty on Barney buying a house in Ireland for Val before the night's over," Chrissie says. "Who's in?"

Wally kisses her hair. "No one's betting against you on this one."

She huffs before kissing his cheek. "I'll be with the women. One of them will take my bet," she says before leaving to join Hailey, Suzie, and Phoebe. No sign of Lexi yet, but I'm positive she'll be here. It's St. Patrick's Day and we're in an Irish pub. She'll show.

Wally scowls at me. "Stop staring at my woman's ass."

"What's with you? You know damn well I'm not staring at Chrissie."

He smirks. "Still mooning over Lexi, eh?"

"Whatever," I mutter before taking a sip of my beer. It – the same as everything else in the bar tonight – is green. In addition to green streamers hung on the walls, there are balloons in various colors of green dangling from the ceiling, and the tables have been covered with green tablecloths with four-leaf clovers on them.

"Did a leprechaun puke in here?" I ask.

Faith comes up behind me and smacks me on the shoulder. "I think it's festive."

"The decorations are awesome, sweetheart," Max says.

"Suck up," I mutter, which earns me another smack from his wife.

We stand around drinking beer and shooting the shit for a while. I speak when spoken to but otherwise, I'm not paying much attention. I can't help my gaze from roving to the door time and time again. Lexi better make an appearance tonight. Otherwise, I'll be showing up at her house and we'll be having a little talk about her avoiding me and her friends.

I notice the time. It's past eight. I'm done waiting. I slam my beer on the bar. Before I can take my first step toward the door, it opens and Lexi strolls in. Her gaze meets mine, but she doesn't hold my gaze. No, she's on the run. She rushes toward her friends as if they can save her. Hasn't she learned anything by now? They're more likely to push us together than hide her.

I capture her hand before she can join her friends. She tries to yank away from me, but I'm not having it. Out of the corner of my eye, I notice Wally walk down the hallway toward the restrooms. Perfect.

"I have something to show you."

She rolls her eyes. "Does that line ever work?"

I waggle my eyebrows. "It does. Once you've seen it, you'll know why."

"Perv."

I chuckle. "Come on. There's no time to waste."

"Uh-oh. Is the little blue pill about to wear off?"

I growl and drag her to the hallway. I pin her to the wall and thrust my hard length into her belly. "I don't need any pill when you're around. This happens anytime you're near." It's true. I turn into a randy teenager whenever she's in my vicinity.

She gasps, but there's no time to fool around. I grasp her hand before dragging her toward the men's room. She drags her feet.

"You seriously don't think we're having a quickie in the restroom, do you?"

As if I'd disrespect her by having sex in a public place. When I finally get Lexi where I want her, I'll need a bed and lots of time to explore her body and do all the things to her I've been fantasizing about since the moment I caught sight of her on Christmas day.

I place my hand over her mouth. "Shush or you'll miss it."

Her nose scrunches in irritation but she doesn't say a word. I position us until we're leaning against the wall across from the entrance to the men's room. When I glance down the hallway, I note Chrissie and Hailey creeping toward us. I place a finger over my mouth to quiet them, and they roll their eyes at me.

The toilet flushes. Any second now. Footsteps sound as Wally approaches the door. The door clicks open, and a leprechaun drops from the ceiling and says *Kiss me, I'm Irish.*

Wally screams before punching out at the leprechaun. When his fist connects and he realizes he's fighting a doll, he scowls before reaching for it. He tugs it away from the contraption holding it to the ceiling and marches toward me. He throws the doll at my feet.

"You'll pay for this, Lenny Walker. Mark my words. You will pay."

"Will he have to pay in gold coins?" Chrissie asks between her giggles of laughter.

"Or maybe in wishes." Hailey laughs. "You going to grant Uncle Wally three wishes, Uncle Lenny? What's your first wish going to be? To no longer be afraid of clowns and lep-rechauns?"

Wally ignores Hailey's taunts and stalks to his wife. "You're going to pay for laughing at me, Angel."

She licks her lips in response. "I am? What are you going to do to me, Mr. Bossy?"

Lexi slams her hands over her ears. "La la la la. I can't hear you. I don't want to hear about my best friend doing the nasty."

Suzie screeches to a halt next to Hailey. She gasps for air before bending over to catch her breath except she can't bend over because her pregnant belly is in the way. She nearly topples over, and Hailey has to grasp her elbow to stop her from crashing to the floor.

"Who is…" she wheezes, "doing the nasty?"

Hailey waits until Lexi drops her hands to answer. "Uncle Wally and Aunt Chrissie in the men's room."

Chrissie's nose turns down. "Um, no. Sorry, Bossy, I am not removing my underwear in there for anyone."

Wally leans down to whisper something into her ear. Her cheeks darken at whatever he has to say. But instead of stealing her away, he kisses her nose and saunters off.

Chrissie waves a hand in front of her face. "The man is dangerous."

"He is? Tell me more," Suzie insists.

There's my cue. I kiss Lexi's hair before following Wally.

As much as I'd enjoy spending the evening breaking Lexi's walls down, a sledgehammer is not going to work in this instance. I'm going to have to break her walls down brick by brick without her realizing it until she's standing in front of me with nothing between us.

Chapter 12

Friends are like melons. To find a good one, you need to try at least one hundred others first.

I GLARE ACROSS THE pub at Lenny. He smirks in response. Ugh. Why won't he leave me alone?

"Maybe if you stopped undressing him with your eyes, he'd leave you alone," Chrissie says.

I frown at her. "I didn't speak out loud."

She points at me and mimes shooting me. "Gotcha! You are totally undressing him with your eyes."

"Am not." Great. I've become a sulky teenager whining to her parents.

"Please, like I don't know what you're thinking by now."

While it's true Chrissie and I have been friends for a long time, we haven't actually spent much time in each other's company. She was out saving the world with weapons strapped to her back while I tried to save the world with a computer. Guess who was more effective? Since the world remains a mess and probably always will be, I'm going with neither of us.

Val arrives and collapses in a chair.

"And? Are you now the proud owner of a home in Ireland?" Chrissie is practically rubbing her hands together. I bet her twenty dollars Barney wouldn't buy them a house in Ireland.

"No," Val huffs.

I hold out my palm to Chrissie. "Pay up, sucker!"

She slaps a bill in my hand. "You done me wrong, Val. You done me wrong."

"Don't blame me. Barney wants us to visit Ireland before we buy a place."

My eyes widen. "Does he have the money to buy a second house?"

"Uncle Barney's loaded," Hailey says. "All the uncles are." She waggles her eyebrows at me. "Is Uncle Lenny looking more attractive now?"

"As if Lexi needs money," Chrissie says, and I glare at her. "What? Is it secret?"

Damn straight, it's a secret.

"Ms. Tightwad made a metric ton of money at her previous job and never spent a dime of it."

Oh, she's talking about my savings from working at the agency. Okay then.

"I'm not a tightwad."

She snorts. "Seriously? You drove a rust bucket around until it literally fell apart. I had to pick you up off the side of Interstate 495 when it broke down. As I recall, the towing company refused to tow it to a garage because, and I quote here, 'the rust bucket isn't worth it'."

I clutch at my non-existent pearls. "How dare you call Penny a rust bucket?"

"Giving the rust bucket a name doesn't mean it's not a rust bucket."

I do the mature thing. I stick my tongue out at her.

"And she lived in a studio apartment," Chrissie tells Hailey.

What is this? Pick on Lexi day? Why did I come out to the bar today? My eyes stray to Lenny. Right. Because otherwise, someone threatened to break my door down and drag me to the pub. He winks at me, and my body wakes up to tell me he can drag me wherever he wants. Um, no. I'm in charge here I remind it.

I wrench my gaze away from Lenny. "What's wrong with a studio apartment?"

"How about it was so tiny you couldn't open the bathroom door if the murphy bed was down?"

"If you hadn't decided you could outdrink me in moonshine games, you wouldn't even know about the murphy bed." I didn't sleep in a murphy bed every day. I didn't live in some miniscule studio. I had a normal bed.

Hailey slams her beer on the table. "I have got to try some of this moonshine. Do have a stash at home? Please, say yes."

As a matter of fact, I do. I would be kicked out of the Mullins family if I didn't have moonshine in my house. Although getting kicked out of the family sounds pretty good to me about now.

Before I can answer, Suzie whisper-shouts, "Hide me!" and tries to slide down the booth under the table except her belly makes it impossible for her to slither to the floor. She gets stuck with her belly wedged under the table.

Hailey sighs before grasping her arm and pulling. Nothing happens. Suzie is good and stuck.

"I thought you were over the klutzy thing since you met and fell in love with Grayson," Hailey mutters.

"This is not a klutz situation. This is 'I forgot how big my belly is'-situation."

I giggle. "And how's that working out for you?"

Hailey pulls harder on Suzie's arm and the beers on the table rattle. She doesn't notice and continues to pull on her arm. Chrissie and I grab our mugs before they can tip over, but Hailey isn't paying any attention to hers.

"Geez. How big is your belly anyway? Are you having triplets? Good grief. Can you imagine the world with three mini-Suzies inhabiting it?"

"I'm having six children."

I gasp. "As in there are six babies in there right now? No wonder your husband is Mr. Overprotective."

"Not all at the same time. I'm not some reality television star. Although, Sextuplets with Suzie does have a certain ring to it." She smiles as she envisions herself as a television star, but her smile dies when she spots her husband making his way to our table. "Son of a dog. Grayson. Get me out of here."

"I'm trying," Hailey grunts and pulls on Suzie's arm again. The table rocks and Hailey's beer mug wobbles before crashing and spilling green beer all over Suzie.

Her eyes light up. "Beer." She's practically drooling. I guess this is what happens when a brewer gets pregnant. She licks at the beer covering her face and sighs. "Yummy."

Grayson arrives at the table, and judging by the scowl on his face, he is not happy. "This is why you shouldn't be allowed outside of the house," he mutters before lifting the table to free his wife.

"I told you. Handcuffs are strictly for sexy times." Suzie sits up in her seat before grabbing her t-shirt and sucking on it. "Yuck. Beer and t-shirt is not a good combination."

"I have an idea," I say to her.

Her eyes light up. "You do? Does it involve sexy times with Uncle Lenny's lance of love?"

I feign gagging. "No. And never say lance of love again."

"How about love rabbit, plumtree shaker, silent flute, doodle, belly-ruffian, brat-getter, bush-whacker, love dart, love staff, Timothy tool, gospel-pipe, bald-headed sailor, tonsil tickler, one-eyed snake, womb broom, womb raider, trouser snake, rumpleforeskin, purple helmeted warrior of love, puff the one-eyed dragon, long dong silver, lap rocket, heat seeking moisture missile, clam hammer, the bone ranger, woody womb pecker—"

Hailey slaps a hand over Suzie's mouth.

"No," Val wails. "Don't stop her. I need to write them all down." Sure enough, Val has her phone out and is jotting down notes.

Hailey ignores Val. "Why do you have a list of euphemisms for dick memorized?"

Suzie mumbles behind Hailey's hand. When Hailey doesn't lift her hand, Suzie licks it. "Gross." Hailey wipes her hand on Suzie's t-shirt.

"Because Mr. Overprotective won't let me go in the brew shack anymore and apparently playing feed the kitty more than three times a day is not in Grayson's wheelhouse."

Grayson growls at her. "I told you. You need to give a man a chance to recover. I'm not eighteen anymore."

Suzie lays her hands on her belly. "I gave you a chance to recover."

"And snuck out of the house to come here."

"I didn't sneak out. It's not my fault you were passed out when I told you I was leaving." She waggles her eyebrows at Hailey. "Pregnancy hormones make you seriously horny. You should try it."

"Unlike you, I don't need to get pregnant to have great sex."

"Me either," Val supplies. She winks over at Barney. "But those pregnancy hormones sound fun. I'd give it a try if I were you, Hailey."

Hailey grunts. "Easy for you to say. Your baby-making factory is closed for good. Mine remains open for business."

Grayson groans. "Please, for the love of beer, do not talk about your baby-making factories in front of me."

"If you can't handle it, leave, Mr. Passes Out After Three Goes."

"Precious, I'm not leaving without you." He holds out his hand.

"Fine, but I want a serving of nachos with extra-spicy jalapenos first." Suzie grips his hand, and he hauls her to her feet.

"The jalapenos give you indigestion."

"But Baby Grayson wants jalapenos," Suzie pouts, and Grayson gives in.

"Ladies, can I steal Lexi away for a minute?"

Crap. Suzie and Grayson's bickering distracted me. I should have been paying more attention to my surroundings and now Lenny managed to sneak attack.

"Of course, Uncle Lenny," Hailey beams up at him.

I don't bother protesting. It's best to get this over with – whatever this is.

Lenny guides me to the hallway.

"What is this? Round two of I have something to show you? Thus far, I'm not impressed."

He snickers before maneuvering me until my back is up against a wall. Shit. How did he manage to outmaneuver me? I'm not drunk. I've only had two green beers.

"Trust me, Whiskey. When the time is right, you'll be impressed," he whispers in my hair. His breath on my neck causes goosebumps to explode on my skin. He bites my earlobe and I have to gather every ounce of willpower I have to stop myself from wrestling him to the ground and having my way with him right here, right now.

I lean back until my body is plastered against the wall as far away from Lenny and his hormone wrecking body as I can get. "What do you want, Lenny?"

"I think we both know what I want."

Yeah, I kind of figured out what he wanted when I felt his hardness pressing up against me. But my momma doesn't call me stubborn for nothing.

"We?" I cock an eyebrow. "I don't want you."

He glides the tip of his nose along mine, and I have to slam my palms against the wall to stop myself from grabbing his head to keep him right where he is.

"Wrong. You don't want to want me. There's a difference."

"There is no difference."

He grins and I hold my breath in anticipation of what he's going to say next. "You need me to drive you home?"

Not the words I expected to come out of his mouth. "Nope. I only drank two beers."

"Good. I'll see you soon," he says and saunters off without looking back.

What in tarnation? He gets me all hot and bothered and then just leaves. Who does he— I slap myself upside the head. *No, Lexi.* You can't have a man, remember? At least not until you straighten out the mess in West Virginia. The mess you've been ignoring.

Chapter 13

A friend calls to check up on you. A good friend shows up and demands you wash your hair and get out of your pj's.

LENNY

Lexi's door flies open, and I shove the cup of coffee into her hands as an offering. "Good morning, Whiskey."

Her eyes narrow on me, but she nabs the coffee. While she sips her drink, I study her. She obviously just rolled out of bed as her hair is sticking up every which way and she's wearing a pair of flannel pajamas. The flannel pj's with hearts on them are adorable, but I'd much rather she ditched the pants to bare her long legs.

"What are you doing here this early on a Saturday morning?" she asks once she's drunk half of the cup of coffee.

"I need your help with the boys."

"Why didn't you say so? Let me get dressed."

I knew she wouldn't hesitate to help if it's for the six kids I coach hockey. She fell in love with those kids straight away. The goofball teenagers are easy to love.

She whirls around, but before she can run away, I snatch her hand to stop her. "Don't you want to know what I need your help for?"

"Nope. If it's for the boys, I'm in."

I use my grip on her hand to draw her near and kiss her forehead. "Thank you."

She scowls at me. "Don't thank me for doing the right thing." I release her and she heads toward her bedroom.

"Wear something you don't mind getting dirty," I call after her. She gives me a thumbs-up before disappearing into her room.

While she gets dressed, I study the interior to check if she's made any changes since I was last here. I smile when I note there are now colorful blankets and pillows decorating the living room. I don't notice any family pictures, but one step at a time. She's slowly settling in. I can't ask for anything more.

Five minutes later, Lexi enters the living room wearing faded jeans and a sweater with a rip in the shoulder showcasing her creamy white skin. Her hair's up in a ponytail and her face is devoid of make-up. Wearing old clothes and with a fresh face, she couldn't be more beautiful, and I can't resist telling her so.

"You're beautiful."

"You need to get an eye exam, old man."

"I have perfect vision." Thanks to laser surgery.

"Whatever. Let's roll."

She doesn't wait for me before grabbing her keys and opening her front door. She motions to me. "Come on. We haven't got all day."

"You don't even know what we're doing today."

"My comment stands. We don't have all day. Get your old man ass moving."

I'm on her before she finishes speaking. I have her plastered to the door with the front of my body touching every delicious inch of hers. "Old man ass? I'll show you my ass and then we'll talk about whether it's an old man's ass."

Her eyes close for a brief second as she shivers. And, because my body is touching hers, I feel her breasts press against my chest. My cock twitches and I have to breathe deeply before I decide to say screw it and spend the day naked with her. Assuming she'd let me.

I shuffle back and grasp her hand. "Who's the slow poke now?"

"More hockey practice?" Lexi asks once we're in my SUV.

"Not today."

"Are you going to tell me what we're doing?"

I wink over at her. "You'll see."

She crosses her arms over her chest and harrumphs. She's adorable with her mouth pursed in a pout and her nose scrunched up. She makes me want to irritate her every chance I get. I don't tell her, though. I enjoy my balls where they are.

We arrive at the lot, and I count heads. Darren, Bran, Malik, Kevin, Jordan, Jayden. Good. All six of my hockey boys are present and ready to work.

"Oooh, Coach Walker brought his girlfriend," Darren taunts and wraps his arms around himself while making kissing noises. "Oh, yes. Just like that. More. More."

"Knock it off." I bump his shoulder.

Meanwhile, Lexi is behind me laughing her ass off. I guess I can put up with a bunch of teenagers being brats if it makes her happy.

I clap my hands to get the boys' attention. "Time to get to work. There are garbage bags and tools in the back of the vehicle."

They trudge off while Lexi studies the abandoned lot with weeds growing higher than my hip. Old tires, overfull trash bags, fast food wrappers, and other trash is strewn across the ground.

"What are we doing?" she asks while the boys unload the supplies.

"We're clearing out this lot."

"Did you buy the lot?"

I did, but I'm not going to brag to her. "We're making a vegetable garden."

"Yeah," Kevin says as he passes. "We're going to sell the vegetables and use the money to buy new hockey gear."

"Wow. What a cool idea."

I wrap my arm around her shoulder and draw her near. "You approve?"

"Approve? Approve is too soft a word. This is awesome. Why don't you call your brothers and have them help? We'll have this lot cleared up in no time."

"No. This has to be a project the boys do. They need to learn the rewards of hard work."

She smiles up at me. "You surprise me, Lenny Walker."

"Coach Walker's in loooove," Brandon crones before clutching his chest and batting his eyelashes.

"You better tie her down as fast as you can, Coach. Otherwise, some other guy is going to steal her away from you," Malik adds.

As if I'd ever let any man get in my way when it comes to Lexi. "Who's going to steal her away?" I ask.

"Probably some guy who's younger than you," he answers.

"Totally," Jordan agrees. "You're beyond ancient. She's a MILF and out of your league."

Lexi coughs to hide her giggle. "Old man," she mumbles under her breath.

"Old man? Who you calling old man?" I tickle her rubs and she swats her hands at me to try to keep me away.

"Stop! Stop! I give in."

I freeze. "You agree I'm not an old man?"

She nods and I remove my hands. "Not an old man. You're ancient," she says before sprinting away from me.

She hides behind Jorden and Malik. Lexi's tall for a woman at five-foot-nine but she squats down behind them. "Protect me from the old guy."

I whistle to get everyone's attention. "Enough fooling around. We have a lot of work to do if we're going to clean up this lot and have it ready for planting by spring. Or don't you want new hockey gear next season?"

The boys groan in unison. "Pair off in groups of two and get to work at removing the garbage."

While the boys rush to do my bidding, I approach Lexi. "Do you know anything about gardening?"

She shrugs. "Not really. Unless you call growing marijuana gardening." Her eyes widen when she realizes what she said. She slaps a hand over her mouth. "Forget I said anything."

"Isn't marijuana legal in West Virginia?"

She studies me for a long moment before answering, "There's a difference between smoking and growing. Besides, all those rules are new. None of them were around when my granddaddy was 'farming' the fields."

Interesting. I knew her family made moonshine, but I didn't realize they were farmers, too. Outlaw farmers at that. I find it hard to believe the law-abiding Lexi comes from a family who flaunts the law, but I'm certain there's more to the story. She doesn't let me ask any questions, though.

"If you tell anyone what I said, I will gut you. And I'll have you know I've been gutting fish since I was old enough to hold a fillet knife."

I have no doubt she could filet me like a fish. But I will never tell her secrets. I palm her neck and bring her near until I can place my forehead against hers.

"Anything you tell me in confidence remains with me. You can trust me."

She narrows her eyes. "You won't tell anyone? Even your brothers?"

"Not even my brothers."

My gaze dips to her lips, and I watch as she licks them. I glance at her eyes to discover them focused on my lips. It's an invitation I can't refuse.

"Get a room," Darren shouts, and I close my eyes with a sigh. Cockblocking teenagers.

I feel the moment Lexi realizes where she is and what she was about to do. She stiffens before jumping away from me.

"Let's get this lot cleared!" she orders as she runs away from me.

I let her. There's only so much I can push her when we're standing in broad daylight on the sidewalk in front of the teenagers I coach. Brick by brick I'll tear her walls down.

Chapter 14

You don't have to be crazy to be my friend. But it helps.

"I don't understand why we have to have two baby showers. One for Suzie now and one for Phoebe in a couple of weeks," I grumble to Hailey as we walk up the sidewalk to Val's house.

"Because Val's crazy and I'm not letting her organize the baby shower for Baby Rossi," Phoebe says as she comes up behind me.

"Sorry, Phoebe. I didn't mean to sound negative."

She winks. "Trust me. After today, you'll understand."

Val opens the door wide. "Welcome to my not so humble abode. Come in. Come in."

I enter and my jaw drops to the floor at the interior of the house. Val wasn't kidding. There's nothing humble about the interior of this house. It's absolutely gorgeous. It's an open plan with two living spaces in the front split by a floating staircase in the middle and a kitchen and dining area in the back. The floors are wide parquet floors, and the trim is oak wood.

A stone fireplace in one living space is lit and next to it sits Suzie on her throne. She's wearing a crown and a t-shirt dress.

The 3D print on the dress is fashioned to appear as if her baby bump is a pouch with a baby trying to escape. Above it are the words 'future brewer'.

"It's Suzie day," Suzie shouts.

"When isn't it Suzie day?" Hailey mutters as she dumps her present on the designated table. She joins Mary Ann, Faith, and Chrissie who are sitting on sofas surrounding Suzie.

I feel my forehead wrinkle as I note the drinks in their hands. "Are you drinking from baby bottles?"

Val shoves a bottle in my hand. It's filled with blue liquid, has a blue and white straw, and is labeled 'it's a boy'.

I squeal. "You're having a boy!"

Suzie smirks. "It's not time to tell yet."

Chrissie holds up her drink. Hers is pink. "When she reveals the baby's gender, those with the correct color bottle win a prize."

"Go boy!" I cheer before sucking down a sip. My stomach revolts. "What is this? Straight up sugar?"

"Isn't it delicious?" Suzie sips from her bottle. Her drink is purple and is labeled 'I'm not telling'.

Val claps her hands. "We can begin since everyone's here now."

I sit down next to Mary Ann on a loveseat across from the fireplace. "Don't worry," I whisper to her. "I brought a flask."

I open my bottle and tip a bit of the moonshine from my flask in. I lift the flask to Mary Ann in question. She holds out her bottle, and I pour a dash of moonshine in.

"I want in on this." Chrissie shoves her pink bottle at me.

"Me too," Hailey agrees.

I end up pouring moonshine into everyone's bottles except for Phoebe's and Suzie's obviously.

"I only want to try it. I do have alcoholic drinks for later." Val motions to the kitchen counter where bottles of champagne are chilling in buckets filled with ice.

"It's handy having pregnant friends. I vote Phoebe and Suzie are our designated drivers," Hailey shouts and thrusts her hand in the air.

"Maybe slow down on the moonshine," I tell her.

"Why? I'm not driving."

"Let's get started, shall we?" Val asks.

"Goodie. Presents," Suzie squeals.

"No." Val wags her finger. "We're playing some games, then we're eating, then you can open your presents."

Suzie huffs and crosses her arms over her belly.

"Our first game is—"

"I thought you were going to announce the sex of the baby and give a prize for those of us with the right color bottle?" Phoebe wiggles her pink bottle. "Come on, Suzie. I know you know the sex of your baby."

Suzie winks. "Actually, I don't."

Val sighs. "A fact she could of mentioned when I told her what games we'd be playing today."

Suzie shrugs. "I want to be surprised."

"Whatever," Val mutters before forcing a smile upon her face. "As I was saying, our first game is feed the baby." She points to her dining room table which is set up with jars of baby food, bibs, and blindfolds.

"You pair off—"

She doesn't finish the words before Chrissie and I stalk to each other. "We're a team."

Phoebe groans. "The super-secret spies are going to kick our asses."

Hailey elbows her. "Where's your competitive spirit?"

Val bangs a spoon against the table. "Stop interrupting and let me explain." She waits for everyone to quiet down before she gives us our instructions. "You'll be blindfolded before attempting to feed each other a jar of baby food," she pauses, "at the same time." I smirk. Chrissie and I are going to kick ass. "The fastest team wins a prize." I catch Chrissie's attention, and she winks in response. We got this.

"Who's first?"

Chrissie and I don't hesitate. We sit down across from each other at the table. I put on my bib before opening the jar of baby food and laying the spoon next to it. I notice Chrissie has done the same as me. I tie my blindfold behind my head and put my hands on the table.

"Ready, set, go!"

I grab the spoon and jar. "You first," I tell Chrissie and open my mouth. The spoon hits my mouth and I lean forward to swallow the mouthful of baby food.

"Now me," I say as I jut my spoon straight forward to where I know Chrissie is sitting.

"They're cheating," Hailey moans.

I'd ask how we're cheating, but I'm busy here.

"Did you check the blindfolds?"

Before Val can answer, I put my spoon down and yell "Done!" simultaneously with Chrissie. I whip off my blindfold and give Chrissie a high-five.

"We might as well declare them the winners and move on to the next game," Mary Ann says. "And maybe something without blindfolds. These two seem to have experience working while blindfolded."

Not exactly. But we have done training while wearing black hoods over our heads. The effect is the same, though.

Val sighs but agrees to skip to the next game. Huh. A baby shower is more fun than I thought. I've only been to one other baby shower in my life, and it was not fun. Not at all. But that's a story for a different time.

Val points to the other end of the table where six baby bottles are lined up. "This is a simple game. Whoever finishes their drink first wins."

Phoebe reaches forward for a bottle, but Val stops her. "This game is strictly for non-pregnant women."

Awesome. Another game I'll win. Hailey narrows her eyes at me. She points to me before mouthing *It's on.* I smirk. It is so on.

Val hands Suzie her stopwatch. "You can time us."

"This is what I get for allowing alcohol at my baby shower. Normally, baby showers are alcohol-free in respect of the soon-to-be mother. But no, I had to tell Val I didn't mind if my guests drank. I thought she meant she'd serve Mimosas or some other type of girly drink. Not have fun drinking games."

Phoebe throws an arm over her shoulder. "You're the one who wants six kids. In order to have six kids, you need to be pregnant a whole lot."

Suzie frowns. "I'm re-thinking the whole six kids thing right now."

I maneuver myself to stand next to Hailey. Chrissie is a stronger drinker, but Hailey's faster. She's my real competition here.

"Are you going to stand there whining and complaining all day or are we going to do this?" Hailey yells at Suzie.

Suzie sticks her tongue out at Hailey before holding up the stopwatch. "Ready, set, go."

As soon as she says go, I snatch a baby bottle from the table. I tilt my head back and commence sucking. The first drop of liquid hits my tongue and I nearly gag. Again, with the sweet shit. I never realized Val had such a sweet tooth. I'm going to need a dentist appointment after today.

I reach up to clamp my nose close. There. Much better. Although I can still taste the sweetness on my tongue, it's less potent since I can no longer smell the sugar. I begin sucking in earnest. I ignore everyone and concentrate on drinking. I don't pause until my bottle's empty.

"There!" I slam my bottle down.

Hailey's a few seconds behind me. "Holy cow. How did you drink that fast?"

I wink. "A woman never tells her secrets."

I go in search of water to rinse my mouth while the other women finish their drinks. They've slowed down now they've lost the race. I swig water from the tap before swirling it around in my mouth and spitting it out.

We play a few more games – bobbing for nipples, decorate the diaper, and guess the baby food flavor. Chrissie and I are tied with three wins each when Val announces it's time for the final game. I elbow Chrissie and mouth *I'm going to kick your ass.*

"Our final game of the day is…" Valerie pauses for dramatic effect. "Who knows mommy best?"

"Yes!" Hailey pumps a fist. "Finally! I'm going to win a game."

I shrug. "You can have this one, Hailey." Don't I sound magnanimous when in actuality I have no chance of winning against Suzie's best friend?

We gather around the fireplace and Val hands us a sheet of paper and pencil each. "No peeking." She slaps Hailey's hand when Hailey attempts to flip the paper over.

"When I say time, you can turn the page over and begin answering the questions. Whoever answers the most questions correctly wins."

Suzie waves her hand. "You forgot to give me one."

Val rolls her eyes. "Duh. Because you know all the answers."

Suzie sticks out her bottom lip. "But I haven't won one game today. Between super-secret spy one and super-secret spy two, no one else has had a chance today."

I point to the table laden with presents. "But you got a whole bunch of presents and you get to open them soon."

"Not to mention you'll soon have a baby, which is the best present of all," Faith points out.

Hailey feigns gagging. "Says you."

Val is done listening to us, which she makes clear when she shouts, "Ready. Set. Go."

I flip over the paper and scan the questions. *What is mommy's favorite color? What is mommy's favorite book? What is mommy's shoe size?* I don't know any of these. I quickly fill out Suzie's name and her birthday and hand my sheet to Val before standing and making my way to the bar.

Chrissie joins me there a few minutes later. I hand her a glass of champagne. "What? Are you out of moonshine?"

I remove my flask and shake it at her. "No. But I'm driving."

She waggles her eyebrows. "You could always call Lenny to drive you home."

"You need to stop. Lenny and I will never happen."

"You need to get over him being bi-sexual. I didn't figure you were this prejudiced."

"I'm not prejudiced. I don't care he's bi-sexual. But the fact he's a man whore? Now, that bothers me."

She snorts. "He hasn't been with anyone since you appeared, and you know it. You're running scared. What I want to know is why? What secrets are you hiding?"

I stare her straight in the eye. "Nothing. I'm not hiding any secrets."

I'm going to burn in hell for lying to my best friend, but I'm not telling her my entire sordid history. She'll have to be satisfied with what she does know. She knows more than anyone else after all. There's no reason to embarrass myself further by baring my past to her.

Chapter 15

I FROWN WHEN I notice Lenny approach where I'm standing in the middle of a park a few weeks later.

"What are you doing here?" I ask when he's within hearing range.

"Suzie asked me to help."

Sigh. Of course, she did.

Suzie organizes an Easter egg hunt every year for mentally challenged children. This year Grayson forbade her from attending since she's heavily pregnant. But no one can forbid Suzie from doing anything. Her husband probably begged and whined and promised sexual favors until she agreed to ask someone to help her out.

She told me she agreed with Grayson because she's feeling tired and doesn't want to slow the kids down. Yeah, right. She had this little matchmaking trick planned all along. I should have known. She probably has Easter in the 'when Lenny and Lexi will burn up the sheets'-pool. Do none of my new friends understand the word boundaries? I think not. Feeling tired, my ass.

"Happy Easter, Whiskey," Lenny says and kisses my forehead.

My skin tingles where his lips linger on it. I force myself to ignore the feeling. No good comes from tingly feelings in my experience.

"One, it's not Easter yet." Easter's next week, but we're doing the Easter egg hunt this week as Suzie was unable to reserve the park location on the day of Easter itself. "And two, friends don't kiss friends foreheads."

He sighs. "Are we back to the whole friend zone malarky?"

"We never left."

Yeah, yeah. I know I sound like a hypocrite since I accidentally kissed Lenny a few times. But kissing does not automatically equal graduation from the friend zone. My friend zone boundaries are reinforced steel concrete and don't crumble after a few kisses. No matter how toe curling his kisses happen to be.

He opens his mouth – probably to argue with me – but he doesn't get a chance to speak before a woman comes rushing over to us.

"Are you Lexi?"

"I am." I point to Lenny. "And this is Lenny. He'll also be helping out."

"Good, you're both here. I'm Dawn."

"How can we help?" I ask with a smile.

"We need to pair the children into groups of two and ensure each group has a basket. One of you should participate in the hunt as well. Suzie usually does, and the kids love it." I should have known Suzie participates. She's a child herself most days.

"We also need someone to finish the gift bags for the children before the Easter egg hunt is done, and we need to prepare lunch for the children and their families so it's ready to be served once the prizes for the hunt are awarded."

"I'll manage the gift baskets and lunch," Lenny offers. "You handle the Easter egg hunt."

I frown. The gift baskets and lunch are big tasks. I should help him instead of hunting for eggs.

We reach the picnic area where the other volunteers are gathered. On the far end are the children. There are probably thirty of them in total. Some are running around in circles while others bounce up and down in excitement. Seeing their excited faces, I can understand why Suzie organizes this event each year. The woman is a pain in my ass, but she's got a soft heart.

I catch Lenny's hand before he can leave. "I can help with lunch or the gift bags."

"It's fine. I've got this. You go have fun with the kids."

I study the tables piled high with gifts needing to be sorted into gift bags. I bite my lip. "You sure?"

Lenny leans close to remove my lip from my teeth. "No abusing my lips."

I want to scowl and remind him of the friend zone, but the feel of his calloused fingers on my bottom lip short-circuits my brain. I step away before I suffer permanent brain damage.

"Go on. The kids are ready." He tilts his chin toward the children.

I follow Dawn over to where the kids are gathered. She hands me a whistle and motions for me to get on with it. I blow the whistle, and the kids immediately freeze.

"Who's ready to have some fun?"

The next minutes are chaos as I group the children into pairs and give them baskets for collecting eggs. When I've got everyone lined up, I blow the whistle again to quiet them down.

"You've got one hour to collect as many eggs as you can find. You ready?"

"We're ready!"

"And go!"

I watch as they race off screaming the entire way. I consider for a moment what could have been – how it would have felt to have my own child here running around searching for eggs – but I immediately force those thoughts out of my mind. Reminiscing about the past will get me nowhere.

Dawn thrusts a basket into my hands. "You better get going or there won't be any eggs left."

"You're serious?"

"As a heart attack."

I grasp the handle of the basket and amble to the nearest tree where I spot several eggs peeking out between the branches. Since I'm tall, I can grasp them without any need to climb the tree. It's not cheating. It's not my fault I'm taller than the kids.

Someone tugs on my jeans. "Those are our eggs." His nametag says he's Brian.

"They are?" I point to his basket. "They're not in your basket, Brian."

His partner, the nametag identifies her as Jenny, shouts, "But we saw them first. Finders, keepers!"

I scan the area to check if anyone is paying attention to us, but there's no one around. "Why don't we split them?" I whisper-shout with a wink.

They jump up and down while screaming yes. I place my finger over my mouth and shush them. "We have to be quiet. We can't let anyone know we're working together."

Once they've mimicked zipping their lips, I pluck the eggs out of the tree keeping half of them for myself. As soon as we've pillaged the tree, they yell their thanks and hurry off. And I don't stare after them getting all nostalgic. Not I.

I force my gaze away from them and scan the area for a good egg hiding place and notice some bushes everyone else is ignoring. Everyone knows bushes are prime Easter egg hiding spots.

As I stroll toward the area, another pair of hunters join me. I raise an eyebrow at the boy and girl before I increase my pace. Their little legs can't keep up with my long strides and they begin to run. Pretty soon I find myself running down the hill toward the bushes in front of them when Smack! An egg hits me in the back of my head.

I turn around to glare at the pair.

"Hurry. Grab the eggs while she's distracted," says the girl. I squint to read her name tag. Rebecca. Game on, Rebecca. Game on.

If they think I'm standing down, they have another thing coming. My momma might call me stubborn, but Papa calls me more competitive than a dang racehorse.

I grab an egg out of my basket and throw it toward them as they rush down the hill. It doesn't hit either one of them. I don't want it to. It sails over them and lands with a thump right in front of them. They freeze, and I use their distraction to start running again.

Rebecca sticks out her leg to trip me, and I start to fall. But I'm not rolling down this hill by myself. I capture her around the waist as I fall, and she falls with me; giggling the entire time.

"Get the eggs, Robby," she orders her partner in between giggles. "Get the eggs."

"I'll get the eggs all right," I grumble as I tickle her.

I hear someone clear his throat and I glance up to find Lenny standing over us. He cocks an eyebrow. "Having fun?"

"She started it." I point at Rebecca who's smart enough to run away while I'm distracted. She grabs Robby's hand and the two of them escape before I can stand up.

Lenny holds out his hand and I let him help me up. I brush my hands over my jeans, now covered in grass stains. He chuckles before reaching over and picking a leaf out of my hair.

"Dawn asked me to come find you to let you know the time's nearly up." He picks up my basket and offers me his arm.

I thread my arm through his elbow as we hike up the hill to the picnic area. "Are the gift bags ready?"

"They are, but I could use some help getting lunch ready."

"What do you need me to do?"

We spend the next ten minutes preparing the lunch by setting out the sandwiches and making vats of lemonade. Afterwards, it's time to announce the winner of the Easter egg hunt and pass out the gift bags. Lenny and I work as a team. Me congratulating each child before he gives them a gift bag.

Once everyone has a gift bag, it's lunchtime. Once again, Lenny and I form a team. He stands next to me as I hand out sandwiches and he scoops piles of potato salad and fruit salad onto plates.

I can't stop myself from smiling over at him. Today is turning out to be more fun than I expected, and I had high hopes for an Easter egg hunt. Sigh. There's nothing more attractive than a man willing to give his time to help children.

Judging by the smirk on Lenny's face, he knows exactly what I'm thinking. Why can't he be a jerk? It would be much easier to live knowing I can't have him if he were a jerk. And, trust me, I can't have Lenny no matter what my body may think. At least, not yet.

Chapter 16

A good friend calls you in jail. A great friend bails you out of jail. A best friend sits next to you in jail and says, "Wasn't that fun?"

LENNY

I enter McGraw's Pub and grin when I observe the table decorated in the middle of the room. Since Faith entered Max's life, his life and our holiday luncheons have become more colorful. Today's Easter luncheon is no different. Faith has decorated the table with bunches of colored tulips and painted Easter eggs.

The woman herself enters the pub, and I give her a hug and kiss. "It looks wonderful in here, doll."

"Thanks. It's our first Easter with the entire family, so I wanted it to be special."

My heart warms at her words. It took Faith a while to accept Max's love, but he persisted and now he finally has the woman he always deserved and a stepson to spoil. The door opens, and Lexi enters. Speaking of persistence.

Lexi's wearing a knee-length flowered dress showing off her long, lean legs. Legs I can't wait to have wrapped around me. Patience, Lenny. Patience.

"Hey, Whiskey," I greet her with a kiss on her cheek.

Her breath catches, and I have to remind myself to be patient again. Easter morning is not the time to throw her over my shoulder and whisk her away no matter how appealing the idea sounds.

"Happy Easter, Lenny, *my friend*."

I chuckle at her emphasis on the words 'my friend'. She can remind me she's put me in the friend zone as much as she wants. We both know I'm busting out of the cage the moment her walls weaken.

"This is awesome," Suzie sings as she arrives.

Lexi narrows her eyes on Suzie. "I knew you had Easter in the pool. I knew it."

Suzie widens her eyes and places a hand over her heart. "Whatever do you mean?"

Lexi snorts. "Whatever."

"Are we betting on when Lenny and Lexi will take the next step in their relationship?" Mary Ann asks as she arrives.

Behind her, Val giggles. "The next step? You mean when Lenny reveals his long dong silver to Lexi."

Suzie holds up her hand, and Val slaps it. Barney chuckles as he throws his arm around Val's shoulders.

"What did the Easter egg say to the boiling water?" He waggles his eyebrows. "I might need some time to get hard. I just got laid by some chick."

I smile at his joke. Barney's been telling dirty jokes since his first wife died. With the way he blamed himself for her death, I was convinced he'd never find another woman. But Val came along with her battering ram, and she rammed and she rammed against his walls until they crumbled to the ground.

I check my watch. It's time. I grab Lexi's hand and tug her outside.

She doesn't pull away, but she does ask, "Where are we going?"

I grin. "You'll see."

Everyone follows us as we exit the pub into the parking lot. A police car is parked on the street and Wally is driving our way. Perfect timing. As soon as Wally passes the squad car, the lights switch on and the siren blares.

"What did you do?" Lexi asks me.

Instead of answering, I get out my phone and hit record.

"You're bad."

Wally pulls into the parking lot and the police vehicle stops behind him. I look through the windshield and notice how pissed Wally is. Meanwhile, Chrissie is covering her face to hide her mirth. Of course, she knows what's happening as I had to enlist her help to ensure Wally would be late arriving this morning. It's no fun pulling a prank if everyone's not there to observe it.

The police officer approaches the driver's window before knocking on it. Wally rolls it down. He waits for the officer to speak but guessing by his red face, it's costing him.

"I'm going to need you to step outside of the vehicle."

Wally hesitates with his hand on the door handle. "I'm sorry, Officer, but can you explain why you pulled me over?"

The officer frowns down at him. "I think the answer to your question would be obvious."

Wally inhales a deep breath before answering. "Could you explain it to me anyway?"

The officer taps his pen on his keyboard as he frowns down at Wally. Most people crumble in no time when trying to stare down Wally. Even I find him intimidating at times. But the officer is holding his own.

Finally, the officer steps back from the driver's door. "I can show you." He motions toward the rear of the vehicle.

Wally exits his vehicle and follows the officer to the rear. I can tell the second he notices the bumper stickers. He swivels his head to glare at our group.

"What is it?" Lexi asks me.

I place my finger over her mouth to quiet her. I want to hear Wally's response to the officer.

"Those aren't mine."

The officer sighs. "I literally cannot count how many times I've heard those three words."

"It doesn't mean anything. Those bumper stickers don't mean I've been smoking and driving under the influence."

The officer frowns. "Sadly. I can't take your word for it."

To Wally's credit, he doesn't argue with the cop. "Fine. Let's do a field sobriety test."

Chrissie gets out of the vehicle and joins our group. I wink at her, and she gives me a thumbs-up. Wally met his match when he married her.

When Wally's attention follows his wife, the officer snaps his fingers in Wally's face. "Put your feet together, hands at the side, and keep your head still." The officer holds up a pen. "Look at the tip of this pen. Follow the movement of the pen with your eyes only. Keep looking at it until I tell you to stop. Do you understand?"

Wally grunts, "Yes."

The cop holds the pen in front of Wally's face and moves it from side to side several times. More than a minute passes, and I notice Wally's hands fist. Someone's getting impatient.

The officer finally sighs and drops the pen. He frowns as he logs the results in his notepad. Wally cranes his neck to read the notepad, and the officer snaps it shut.

"Let's continue, shall we?"

The officer doesn't wait for Wally's response before pointing to the painted line of a parking spot.

"Put one foot in front of the other, walk heel-to-toe, do not step off the line, keep your arms at your sides, and count out loud from one to nine as you take each step, looking at your feet. After the ninth step, pivot on your front foot and return to taking heel-to-toe steps back to the beginning."

The instructions are rapid fire. If Wally didn't know the walk and turn drill already, he wouldn't be able to follow the instructions, which is the point.

"Do you understand these instructions?"

Wally nods, and the cop motions for him to begin.

Wally executes the drill perfectly. He doesn't stumble once. I'm impressed.

"Final drill," the officer says once Wally completes the walk and turn. "Raise one foot off the ground at least six inches. Point the toes of the raised foot toward the ground, keep your arms at your side, your eyes on your raised foot, and count out loud from one to thirty."

Wally lifts his left leg and begins counting. "One, two, three, four, five, six, seven, eight, nine, ten, son of a bitch." He stumbles and his foot touches the ground.

The officer reaches behind him for his handcuffs. "I'm sorry to say, sir, but you've failed the field sobriety test. I'm going to have to ask you to come with me."

"You know damn well the one leg stand is impossible whether you're sober or not."

"But your pupil sizes are not the same either."

"My pupil sizes are not the same? Are you kidding me?" Wally's nostrils flare as he glares at the police officer.

Time to stop this before Wally decks a cop and we have to bail him out of jail on Easter. I hit stop on the recording and stow my phone in my pocket before joining Wally and the officer.

"Ted," I say and extend my hand.

"Lenny. Happy Easter."

As soon as we shake hands, the rest of the group joins us.

"What's on the bumper sticker?" Lexi asks. She giggles when she sees the two bumper stickers. *Weed is legal in my house* and *Stay blazed.*

"I don't know, Wally. These are pretty suspicious in a state that hasn't legalized marijuana yet," Lexi tells Wally.

I wrap an arm around her and drag her away before he thinks he can lash out at her. "Lexi, this is Ted, Darren's dad."

"Ah, now I know how you arranged this little stunt."

Ted smiles. "Anything for the man who managed to get my boy to stop hanging around the gangs and playing hockey instead." He chuckles. "I can't believe you got those teenage boys to plant a vegetable garden."

His radio squawks. He pauses to listen for a second. "Duty calls." He salutes Lenny before returning to his vehicle. He hits the sirens and blasts out of the parking lot.

As soon as the vehicle is gone, Wally turns on Lenny. "What the hell did I do to you to earn this?"

I shrug. He's teased the crap out of me about Lexi is what he's done. But I won't call him out for it when I've got my armed wrapped around her.

"Sleep with one eye open, brother. One eye open," he grumbles and marches away.

"I always do, brother," I call after him.

Lexi giggles and I look down at her. Her face is glowing with happiness. It's worth Wally's considerable wrath to make her happy. If I didn't already know how deep I'm in with Lexi, I would now.

Chapter 17

We'll be friends forever because you already know too much.

THE PHONE IS RINGING when I unlock the door to the PI office on Tuesday morning. I drop my bag on the floor and rush to answer it. "*You Cheat, We Eat,* how may I help you?"

A man grunts into the phone. "Is this the idiot PI firm owned by girls?"

Girls? I bristle. We're not girls. We're women. Hear us roar.

"*You Cheat, We Eat* is operated by professional women."

He snorts. "Professional women? Yeah, right."

I want to hang up on the guy. To be perfectly accurate, I want to reach through the phone and tear his face off. If there's anything that pushes my berserk button, it's condescending men belittling women.

I grit my teeth and do my best to keep my voice pleasant when I ask, "Is there something I can help you with?" Besides a personality change?

"You need to get your noses out of my business."

I'm officially lost and confused. "What business would that be?"

Phoebe and Hailey enter the room laughing. I hold up a hand to quiet them.

"It's my business, not yours."

Wow. He cleared things right up for me. Not.

"Let's try this again. Can I have your name?"

"My name?" He snarls. "I'm not telling you my name."

"I'm afraid it's going to be awful hard to stay out of your business if I don't know who you are," I explain calmly as I roll my eyes in Hailey and Phoebe's direction.

"Mind your own business," he yells and disconnects.

"Who was it?" Hailey asks when I hang up the phone.

"No clue. He wouldn't tell me his name," I state before explaining the phone call.

"Most likely some dude who got caught with his pants down and now has to pay child support."

Hailey's probably right. After all, the bulk of her business is finding cheating spouses. I nearly ask her how she manages to encounter the filth of humanity over and over again and stay a pleasant person, but I stop myself when I realize how hypocritical the question would be coming from me. Like I didn't spend the past twenty some years wading through the worst humanity has to offer.

"Why do men think it's okay to cheat?" Phoebe asks. "If Ryker cheats on me, I'm unmanning him."

"Princess," the man himself says as he comes up behind her and wraps an arm around her. "Why would I cheat when I have you to come home to?" She melts into his arms.

"I thought you were going after a skip today?" I ask Ryker, but Phoebe answers.

"He refuses to leave me alone. Apparently being pregnant has turned me into a simpering woman in need of a man to protect me."

It's actually kind of sweet he's being ultra protective of her, but I keep my thoughts to myself. Unlike Ryker, I can't whisper sweet nothings into Phoebe's ear if she gets mad at me.

The door crashes open. I look past Ryker and Phoebe. Crap on a cracker. My worst nightmare has arrived. My stomach twists and my heart drums in my chest. I'll be damned. I guess you really can't escape your past.

I force out a breath and get my heart rate under control before standing. I cross my arms over my chest and glare at the new arrival. "What are you doing here?"

"You ain't answering my calls or messages. What did ya expect to happen?" Is it too much to pray he'd leave me the hell alone?

"How did you find me?"

He smirks. "Were y'all trying to hide?" Obviously.

I hear a phone beep and notice Hailey's on her phone calling someone. Son of a dog. I forgot I have an audience here.

"Let's go." I stomp around my desk.

Before I can reach him, Ryker blocks me. "Are you okay, Lexi? Do you need me to handle this guy for you?"

"I'm good." Lies. All lies. "Thanks for asking."

He studies me for a moment before moving out of my way. "You know where to find me if you need me."

I don't bother responding. Of course, I know where to find him. His office is literally a door away from my desk. I grab my unwelcomed guest by the upper arm and drag him out of the office and down the hall.

When he opens his mouth to speak, I hiss at him, "Not here."

He smirks and I'm tempted to slap the expression clear off his face. What does he have to smirk about? Does he think he's won since he found me? Not likely.

This is merely the beginning of the fight. I put up with this mess for years. But I knew I had to put a stop to it when I met Lenny. It's not fair to him or me to continue this way. I won't be backing down anytime soon.

We travel with the elevator to the ground floor and exit the building. Once we're on the sidewalk, I spin around to confront him.

"Why are you here? What do you want?"

"I know what I don't want – a divorce."

My stomach dips at his words. I knew when I had my lawyer send him the divorce papers, there was a good chance he wouldn't cooperate. It's why I've been ignoring all his calls for the past months. I thought if I ignored him for long enough, he'd give in. I forgot his stubbornness rivals mine.

"Why? We haven't lived together in two and a half decades."

He frowns. "Y'all know why."

Yeah, I do. "You can have it all. I don't want it."

"Y'all know dang well and good y'all's family won't let me keep the land unless we stay married."

Thus, the reason I've been ignoring the calls from my family. But I am done letting my family rule my life. I shouldn't have let it go on this long as it is. It's utterly ridiculous to be stuck in an arranged marriage after all this time. It's the twenty-first century for crying out loud.

"Don't you want to be married to someone you love? Isn't Ellie tired of being your hot piece on the side?"

He dips his chin. "Ellie don't pay no mind to the arrangement."

Someone sucks at lying. "What about the kids? Don't you want them to have the Harper last name?"

"They do."

My eyes widen. This is news to me. "You claimed them?"

He shrugs. Those poor children. They shouldn't be caught up in all this bullshit.

"You do realize I asked for a no-fault divorce. I could ask my lawyer to re-file the papers and claim it's your fault our marriage didn't last. I could demand spousal support."

I'm talking out of my ass. I have no idea if what I'm saying is true, but one thing I do know is true. It's William the ass's fault the marriage is over.

"There ain't no reason to be cruel, darlin'."

"Me?" I point to myself. "I'm the one who's being cruel? You want to talk about being cruel, do you?"

He holds his hands up in a placating gesture. "I didn't mean …"

"You didn't mean what? You're not a lying, cheating sack of crap?"

"Y'all ain't being fair."

"How's this for what's not fair?" I mutter and step closer. "What's not fair is not being able to tell people the truth. What's not fair is not being able to have a serious relationship with a man."

"Y'all can have a relationship with a man. I ain't stopping ya."

I throw my arms in the air. "Do you not realize how deranged you sound right now?"

William runs a hand through his hair. "Why now? Y'all didn't make no problem with this last time ya was in the holler for Christmas."

Buy a clue, dude! It's been years since I was home for Christmas.

"I've never been fine with this arrangement," I explain. "Did I put up with it? Yes, I did. I shouldn't have. I should have never agreed to it in this first place."

"Y'all was the one who wanted to leave."

"I was always going to leave. You're the one who stopped me from leaving in the first place."

I'm such an idiot. I should have never gone to the bar in town when I was back home celebrating my graduation from college. And I should have definitely not agreed to a drinking game with William and his friends. I may be able to drink Chrissie and her friends under the table, but the boys back home in the holler are a different matter altogether.

William hit on me all through high school. I was never interested. I wasn't interested in boys in general. I was too busy studying and getting good grades – determined to win a scholarship to college since my parents would never finance the studies for me, a mere girl, to go out of state for school – to pay any attention to boys.

Big mistake. William saw me as a challenge and the boy never could back down from a challenge. And I ran headfirst into his snare that day at the bar. All it took was one mistake to ruin my life.

A car screeches to a halt. I glance over to discover it's Lenny's SUV. Great. As if things aren't already a shit show. Lenny climbs out of his vehicle and marches to us.

"Now I get it," William snickers, and my hands fist.

I should deck him. No jury in the world will convict me of assault when they hear the entire story.

Chapter 18

I don't need a psychiatrist to pry into my personal life and make me tell them all my secrets. I have my friends for that.

LENNY

I speed all the way from my place to Hailey's building. When she called to tell me a man showed up at the office of *You Cheat, We Eat* to confront Lexi, my heart stalled in my chest. Lexi in trouble? Not on my watch. I didn't wait for Hailey to finish explaining before hanging up and jumping in my SUV.

I skid through the corner to find Lexi and some man screaming at each other on the sidewalk in front of Hailey's office building. Son of a bitch. What is going on? I didn't detect any danger in Lexi's life.

Of course, I didn't ask Wally to do a full background check on her either. He assured me no one from her work life was after her and I left it there. I'm an idiot. Chrissie also worked at the agency. And she was the furthest thing from safe as a woman on American soil can be.

I screech to a halt in front of them and jump out of my truck.

"What's going on? Who is this guy?" I ask Lexi as I approach.

"I'm William, her husband."

I wait for the punchline, but Lexi doesn't contradict him. What the hell is going on here?

"This guy is your husband?" Please say it isn't true.

She frowns. "We're separated."

"Not by the law," the man sings.

She glares at him. "Stop being an asshole. Do you want me to call Ellie and tell her I'm reneging on the deal?"

"Who's Ellie?"

"His live-in lover and the mother of his children."

What the hell?

"Hold on. He lives with another woman and has children with her, but he's married to you?" This conversation is making things about as clear as mud.

"On paper. It's part of the deal." Lexi's doing an awesome job of not explaining.

"Deal? What deal?"

"It's complicated."

Complicated is code for 'you're not going to be happy with the answer'. Guess what? I'm already not happy – as in pissed – to find Lexi has a husband. Why didn't she tell me? Even if I am firmly stuck in the friend zone, being married is the kind of personal information you tell your friends.

I study William. He doesn't appear to be her type. His hair under his ballcap is long and greasy, his beard is dirty and growing out of control, and his clothes are full of holes. Of course, what do I know about Lexi's taste? Until five minutes ago, I didn't know she was married.

As I stand there trying to figure out how I missed this, someone bumps into me. Crap. We're not alone out here. This is not a conversation we should be having outside where anyone can see and hear us.

"Let's go somewhere private to discuss things," I suggest.

"I need to work, and he has nothing to say I want to hear," Lexi says.

"We need to discuss this."

I frown. What's William talking about? Is 'this' their marriage?

"I don't want to discuss anything with you. I don't want to see your face again."

The fist around my heart loosens and relief pours through my body. Lexi is not in love with this man. Her love for him isn't the reason she's been holding back from me.

I study Lexi's stance. She's not gazing at William with longing in her eyes. She's curling her lip as if his mere presence disgusts her. If he disgusts her, why is she married to him? What am I missing here?

I place my hand on the small of Lexi's back and steer her toward the coffee shop down the street. William glares when he notices the placement of my hand, but Lexi's not having it.

"Don't you dare start with me. How old is your oldest boy now? Fifteen? You can't go all 'She's my woman and beat your chest' when you've been living with Ellie for twenty years."

He's been living with another woman for twenty years? I file the information away for perusal at a later time.

"Soon's y'all move home, Ellie's gone."

Lexi screeches to a halt. "What is wrong with you? Did your momma drop you on your head as a child?" She lifts a hand to stop him from replying. "No, don't answer. I know your momma. She dropped you more than once."

"Doncha dare talk smack about my momma."

Lexi's on a roll and ignores him. "And whatever gave you the idea I'd move back home? I am never moving back to the holler where barefoot and pregnant is all the fashion for women. Never, ever."

"Y'all make us out to be a bunch of hicks."

She snorts. "If the shoe fits…"

"Ain't ya from the holler same as me?"

"And I got the hell out of there as soon as I could."

"What's the holler?" I interrupt their tit for tat to ask.

"Didn't you watch the television show *Justified*?"

I have no idea what she's talking about. I shake my head.

"It's a narrow mountain valley where the roads dead-end and you step back into time to when women were seen as baby making machines and men think it's okay to order women around."

I growl, and she pats my arm. "Not literally." She pauses. "Usually."

If William took a hand to Lexi, I will make him regret the day he was born.

"He never hit me. Half the time he forgot I existed." Hurt flashes in her eyes for a second before she blinks, and it's gone. Maybe I was wrong. Maybe she does love this asshat.

"I said I was sorry for that day a million times. Do y'all have to bring it up every time we're together?"

"Duh. I will never forgive you for what happened. It's my right as a woman to rub it in your face every chance I get. Consider yourself lucky I don't live in the holler."

Did William betray Lexi? Is that what they're talking about? If so, the guy's a complete idiot. You don't cheat on a woman of Lexi's caliber. You worship the ground she walks upon.

I open the door to the café and steer Lexi toward an empty table in the rear. I wait for William to sit down before I drag her down the hallway toward the rear exit.

"What?"

I spin around and pin her to the hallway. "Did he cheat on you? Do you need me to kick his ass?"

She rolls her eyes. "If anyone's going to kick his ass, it's going to be me."

I pinch her chin. "You didn't answer my question."

"It's complicated."

I'm starting to hate the word complicated.

"I've got all day."

"Speaking of which, can you stop by the office and let Hailey know I'm taking my lunch break now? If there's anything she needs me for, she can call me."

I frown. "Are you trying to get rid of me?"

She widens her eyes and bats her eyelashes. "Too obvious?"

I move my hands to cradle her face. "I want to be here with you to support you."

"You also want to hear all about my sordid past."

I don't deny it. "Caught red-handed." I clear my throat. "But I didn't lie. I do want to support you." Someone needs to stand by her side to ensure her so-called husband treats her right because from what I've heard thus far, the man doesn't have a clue how to treat a woman.

"I can't, Lenny." Her words cause the fist around my heart to tighten once again. "It's bad enough I have to deal with William. I don't want my dirty laundry aired for everyone to witness."

"I don't give a shit about your dirty laundry."

She cocks an eyebrow.

"Okay, I do. I want to inspect all your dirty laundry. I haven't made a secret of how I feel about you. It shouldn't surprise you I want to know everything there is to know about you especially when your *husband* shows up."

At the word husband, anger flares in her eyes. But as quick as it flares, she extinguishes it. She's hiding from me, and I don't like it one bit.

"And I haven't made a secret of how I don't want more than friendship with you."

I growl. "Don't lie to me."

"Have I or have I not repeatedly told you you're in the friend zone?"

"Whiskey, your words say one thing, but your body says another."

The door to the kitchen bangs open and a waitress exits carrying a large tray. "Excuse me," she says as she presses past us.

Lexi uses the distraction to push me away.

"Go." She points to the exit. "We'll talk later."

I don't budge. I'm not leaving her with *him*.

"Please," she pleads. "I promise we'll talk later."

"You promise?"

"If you leave now and don't sit outside in your truck watching over my safety, I promise I'll talk to you later."

"Talk to me about him," I clarify.

She huffs. "Yes."

"Okay." I kiss her forehead before she can walk away.

I wait until she's seated at the table with William before I retreat. I retrieve my phone and call Ryker. I need someone to watch over her while she's talking to her fucking husband. How did I not know she's married? It's past time to talk to Wally.

Chapter 19

*If I have to clean my house before you come over,
then we're not real friends.*

I WAIT UNTIL LENNY drives away before addressing the man sitting across from me. "All right. You've got me here. What do you have to say?"

"Y'all need to come home," William announces.

Not going to happen. "I am home." To my surprise, the words ring true.

I came to Wisconsin after I quit the agency because Chrissie was here. I honestly didn't expect to stay. I needed somewhere soft to land where I could figure out my next move. My next move will never, ever be to return to West Virginia.

And there's no way William figures in my future at all. I can't believe he thinks otherwise. We've seen each other maybe twice a year since I left the holler. And those 'reunions' weren't exactly what anyone would call pleasant. Awkward and forced are the words I'd use.

But Milwaukee is starting to feel like home. When did this happen? I fear a sneaky man who refuses to stay in the friend zone has something to do with my feelings. But Lenny isn't the only reason this city feels comfortable. There's Chrissie and all her crazy friends as well.

I'm surprised they haven't shown up yet. I scan the café and my gaze finds Ryker leaning against the wall in the hallway leading to the rear exit. I should have known Lenny wouldn't leave me here alone. And the warmth his protectiveness causes isn't comforting. Not at all.

William sneers. "Y'all can't possibly want to live here."

"What's wrong with here?"

"It's a city. They're dirty and full of crime."

I bark out a laugh. "Because there's no crime in the holler?"

"Growing marijuana and making moonshine ain't no crimes."

I snort. "Law enforcement would beg to differ with your opinion."

I sound bold and certain of myself, but truth be told, law enforcement in the holler knows exactly what the Harpers and Mullins are up to, and they let us get on with it. Us? There is no us. My name may be Mullins, but I do not belong to them. Not any longer.

"Your parents sent me here to bring you back."

I cross my arms over my chest and lean back in my seat. "I guess you didn't tell them about the divorce papers."

He shrugs. "Ain't no reason to. We ain't fixin' to get divorced."

My arms drop, and I lean forward to hiss in his face, "We are getting divorced. You can do this the hard way or the easy way, but it's happening."

"What about the deal?"

I slam my hands down on the table. "I don't give a flying hoot about the deal!"

I barely have a chance to finish my sentence when Ryker appears. "Everything okay here?"

William glares at him. "Who's this? Ya got more admirers? Little miss innocent Lexi ain't no more."

How dare he! Who the hell does he think he is? Oh, yeah. That's right. He's the one who took my innocence when I was drunk on moonshine. My nostrils flare, and my fingernails dig into the table while I battle to keep my temper under control.

"I have no problems hiding his body, but you can't kill him here in front of a dozen witnesses," Ryker tells me.

"You'd hide a body for me?"

He doesn't hesitate to reply. "Of course. You're Phoebe's friend."

"She's the luckiest woman in the world to have you."

He smiles. "Nope. I'm the luckiest man in the world to have her."

William snaps his fingers in front of my face. "Pardon me. Can all y'all stop with the lovey dovey shit now? We got matters to discuss."

"You good?" Ryker asks.

I nod. "I'm good."

He points to the hallway. "I'll be right there if you need me."

To my surprise, I don't bristle at his announcement. It's nice to have someone at my back while I deal with these problems.

Someone who – unlike Lenny – won't pry into what's going on here.

"Y'all need to come home and honor your part of the deal."

The deal. My nostrils flare. I'm about tired of hearing the word 'deal'. I am tired of spending my entire life paying for one tiny mistake. I'm done with it.

"I'm not coming home. I'm divorcing you."

I scoot my chair back to leave, but William grabs my hand to stop me.

"You can't do this. Y'all gave your word." He smirks. "Or is y'all's word no longer good?"

I bristle but I don't take the bait. Doubting a person's word is the worst thing you can do in the holler. "It's been over twenty years. I'm done with this."

"If we get divorced, things'll go right back to the way they were twenty-five years ago."

I cock an eyebrow. "Are you kidding me? You've worked side by side with the Mullins for over two decades now."

When I agreed to marry William, it was with the understanding the rivalry between the Mullins family and Harper family would finally end.

When I came home after that fateful night I spent in William's bed, I figured my parents would disown me for having slept with the enemy. To my surprise, they jumped at the chance to create an alliance between the two families.

According to the deal, if I married William Harper, he received a tract of the Mullins land. In return, the Harpers agreed to stop setting our crops on fire and pouring cases of our moonshine into the river.

When I ran away from William, I knew I couldn't divorce him without all hell breaking loose between the families. So, I carried on knowing William was back home doing whatever he wanted while married to me. But I'm done living this way.

"The Harpers'll see our divorce as a declaration of war by the Mullins."

I bury my face in my hands. This is unfair. Why is my marriage the one thing keeping the holler from exploding into flames? Our marriage isn't even real, except for on paper.

I lift my head. "You need to talk to your family and explain how our divorce has nothing to do with the rivalry between the families."

He snorts. "Our marriage is why the rivalry ended. Of course, our divorce has everything to do with the rivalry."

"I don't care." My heart squeezes at those words. It's not in my nature to place myself first in front of my family, but don't I have the right to come first for once in my life?

William tries another tactic. "Your parents are expecting your return any day now."

"Why?"

I'm genuinely confused. My parents are no strangers to how I feel about living in the holler because I made no mystery of my intentions to leave as soon as I could. They teased me my entire childhood about being a nerd and studying. I didn't care. I knew a scholarship was the only way I'd be able to attend college, other than the local community college.

"Y'all's fun is over. It's time to return home and fulfill your obligations."

"My fun? Are you serious? I haven't been out gallivanting the world."

Thanks to him I might add. The agency was perfectly happy to give me an analyst position, but I could never become a field operative because of my family background. I thought Chrissie came home to West Virginia with me because she was my friend. Nope. She was ordered to use our friendship to learn as much as she could about my family.

When Chrissie first confessed, I was furious. But after she told me she'd report my family was no threat to me, I softened. Eventually, I forgave her.

"You've been living in the big city. Who knows what you've been up to?"

And I'm done talking.

"Are you going to sign the divorce papers or not?"

"I ain't."

I stand. "In that case, you'll be hearing from my lawyer."

"I ain't gonna let you divorce me, Lexi."

I sigh. "Of course, you won't. You've never once given me what I needed or been there for me."

He winces at my words. "Ain't nothin' I can do will change what happened that night."

"And nothing you can do will get me to forgive you."

Ryker sidles up to me. "You ready to go, Lexi?"

"Yep, I'm done here."

He places his hand on my lower back and leads me out the back door of the café. When we reach the alley, he stops.

"Do you need to go somewhere to get rid of your anger before we return to the office? We can hit up the shooting range or I can drive you to the fight gym."

I close my eyes and take a few deep breaths. Breathe in. Breathe out. And repeat. I do this several times until my heart rate returns to normal.

I open my eyes to find Ryker staring at me with concern. I pat his chest. "I'm okay, big guy. I've been dealing with this for more years than I can count. But thanks for your concern."

He grunts. I guess the no talking Ryker has returned.

"Let's get back to work before Hailey sends out the cavalry."

Because she would. And since her cavalry includes Lenny, I could do without it.

Chapter 20

Why can't you be friends with a squirrel? They drive everyone nuts.

LENNY

I enter McGraw's Pub and march to the bar where Max, Wally, Sid, and Barney are congregated. The drive to the bar from the café where I left Lexi with her *husband* hasn't calmed me down. To be honest, I haven't bothered trying to calm down. I'm nursing my anger at this point.

"I need a full background on Lexi," I order Wally. He may be retired from his black ops position, but I know he has the connections I need to dig deep into Lexi's life.

"Well, hello to you too," he replies.

"This isn't the time to be flippant. Lexi's husband showed up at *You Cheat, We Eat* today."

The chatter dies down, and Max switches off the music.

"What did you say?" Wally's question echoes in the now quiet bar.

"You heard me." I'm not saying the words Lexi and husband in the same sentence again. At least, not until her husband is me. I grit my teeth. How the hell did I not know she was married?

"Lexi's married?" Sid asks.

"Holy crap. I did not see this coming," Max grumbles.

"How is a wife like a freezer?" Barney jokes.

I wrap my hand around his neck and squeeze. He claws at my arm, but I can't even feel his nails digging into my skin. "This is not a joking matter." He sputters. "Nod if you understand." He nods, and I release him.

"Huh." Max crosses his arms over his chest. "I've been waiting to hear what kind of trouble Lexi's in. This is not what I expected."

"What gave you the impression Lexi's in trouble?"

Did I miss a clue somewhere? Was I so busy trying to convince Lexi to take a chance on me, I was blind to what was happening right in front of me? And here I thought I'd learned from all the mistakes my brothers made while they were claiming their women.

Max shrugs. "Since this group of men can apparently only attract women who are in trouble, I assumed the same was true with Lexi."

He's not wrong. Faith was in trouble with a gang in Saint Louis when she met Max. Val got caught in the crosshairs of a crime syndicate before Barney took care of the situation. And Chrissie had a stalker when Wally stepped in.

Sid clears his throat. "Mary Ann wasn't in trouble when we met."

"No, but you were."

Sid met Mary Ann when he was burned in a fire Phoebe's ex-husband set to distract us. He took one look at the nurse tending to his wounds and fell hard. After five previous attempts, Sid has finally met his perfect match. I couldn't be happier for him, but I don't want to talk about how all of my brothers have found their perfect matches right now.

"Can you do a background check?" I ask Wally. "A full background check this time?" He raises an eyebrow in response. Shit. He's going to make me beg. "Please."

He grins. "Already did."

Of course, he did. Wally is a bit overprotective when it comes to his wife, Chrissie. I should have realized he'd run a check on Lexi since Chrissie and her are close friends.

"Why didn't you tell me?"

"You never asked."

I did ask. Wait. No, I didn't. I asked if she was in trouble from her past job. Damnit. I didn't realize I needed to be specific with him.

"What did you find?"

Wally gives Max a chin lift. "Can you get Lenny a drink?"

This is not a good start. I repeat my question. "What did you find?"

Wally scratches his chin. "Maybe you should sit down."

Now, he did it. I wrap my hand around his neck and shove him up against the bar. I feel his nine mm thrust against my stomach, but I'm not concerned he'll actually shoot me. He's just showing me he won't go down easily. Tell me something I don't know.

"Stop messing with me and tell me what I want to know."

"I'm trying to calm you down before I tell you," he grits out.

Barney chuckles. "How's that working out for you?"

"Maybe now is not the time to poke the dragon," Sid tells him.

"Nah. I'm safe. He's too busy trying to choke out Wally to bother with me."

Max elbows his way in between us. He squeezes my shoulder until I feel the sting of pain and release Wally. "You. Sit down."

"And you." He frowns at Wally. "You couldn't resist, could you?"

Wally shrugs. "It was getting boring around here."

Sid chuckles. "Chrissie not keeping things exciting for you? I can give you some pointers in the bedroom."

I am done with my brothers not taking this situation seriously. How dare they disrespect me this way.

"Enough!"

At my shout, everyone finally shuts the hell up.

"This is a serious situation with my woman. I didn't laugh and joke when your women were in danger, did I? No, I offered to help without question."

"*Your* woman?" Wally cocks his eyebrow.

"I don't give a shit she's married to the asshat, she's mine."

"That's all I needed to know."

Fucker. He couldn't ask. He had to test me? I debate choking him again, but he can't give me the answers I need if my hand is blocking his windpipe.

Sid pats my shoulder, and we sit down at our usual table. Since there are no other customers, Max joins us.

"Tell me," I order Wally.

"You're not going to be happy, brother."

"No shit. I just met Lexi's husband. Something I was unprepared for because of you."

"You didn't ask." I glare at him until he sighs. "But I should have told you."

"Yeah, you should have."

"I have to warn you," he begins. "I didn't find out much."

"Any information you have is useful." Since I have zero information at this point.

"To start with, Lexi's record is clean." He already told me this part. "I dug a little deeper and discovered she's been married to one William Harper for twenty-five years."

I nod. I know this much.

"Brother, I hate to tell you this, but William Harper is living with another woman, and they have two children together."

"Her name's Ellie. Their oldest child is fifteen."

He cocks a brow. "She told you?"

I shrug. Not exactly.

"When I found out she was married, but no one knew about it, I went deeper and discovered the two have not been in contact until three months ago. Since then, he's called or messaged her several times a day."

I figured he was the reason behind Lexi's phone blowing up constantly.

"Did she tell you why he suddenly showed up after all this time?"

I don't answer. I have no answer. Lexi hasn't opened up to me at all. And here I thought I was breaking down her wall brick by brick. I didn't realize the first wall is merely protecting the inner wall.

"I dug as deep as I could, but I couldn't find out why he's suddenly interested in her."

Damn. I'm going to have to push Lexi for answers. Answers she isn't going to give up easily.

"But, brother, there's something else."

What now? I motion for Wally to continue.

"Before Lexi and William married, the area of West Virginia they lived in was a warzone with two clans fighting for dominance over the marijuana and moonshine trade. Once they married, crime in the area settled down. Violent crimes I mean. The marijuana and moonshine trade continues to rage on."

I rub my jaw. "Lexi said something about a deal."

"Do you think her marriage was part of peace negotiations between the two families?" Sid asks.

"I don't know, but I'm going to find out."

"Val is going to love this shit. She's addicted to those mob movies," Barney says.

"You can't tell Valerie what's happening," I order him.

He chuckles. "As if the women aren't going to invade Lexi's house and force her to tell them all her secrets."

I frown. He's right. They probably will. Lexi won't be happy about it either.

"The question is what are we going to do about this?" Max asks.

"Obviously, we're going to take care of Lexi and make sure her husband leaves her alone," Sid offers.

I stand. "But first we need to have all the information. I'm going to talk to Lexi."

"Go easy on her, brother," Barney yells after me.

I give him a two-fingered wave. I can't promise to go easy. Not after she's lied to me for the past months. Married?!

Chapter 21

Why did the zombie ignore all his Facebook friends? He was still digesting all of his followers on Twitter.

I SIGH WHEN I hear the knock on the door. I swear if William found out where I'm living, I'm going to drag him into the backyard and make him dig a ditch before throwing him in it. Wally won't mind if I dig up his yard. Not when he hears the story. What am I saying? It's Wally. He probably already knows the story.

The knock on the door changes into pounding. I stomp to the door and peek through the spyhole. When I spot who's standing there, I fling the door open.

"What do you want, Lenny?"

He doesn't bother to answer as he pushes past me inside the house.

"What are you doing? It's not okay to invade my house."

He whirls on me. "You promised to talk later if I left you alone at the café."

I cross my arms over my chest. "But you didn't leave me alone at the café, now did you?"

He marches to me and pinches my chin to ensure he has my undivided attention. "If you think for one second I would leave you alone with someone you obviously don't want to spend time with, then you don't know me at all."

I deflate. He's right. I knew he'd send someone to babysit me while I spoke with William. There's no sense denying it. At least he didn't send one of his brothers. Those former military men gossip more than a bunch of old women doing laundry down at the crick.

Great. I spend less than an hour in William's presence and I'm using West Virginia slang.

Lenny's hand glides from my chin to cradle my cheek. "Whiskey, I can't protect you if I don't know what's going on."

I close my eyes and lean into his touch for a moment. Wouldn't it be nice if I had someone to support me through this? Someone I could lean on. But I don't. I straighten and step away.

"There's no need to protect me. I'm not in any danger."

He grunts before snatching my hand and dragging me to the sofa. "Why did your husband show up now? Is he the one who's been blowing up your phone after two decades of nearly nothing?"

I rub my temples where I feel a killer headache blossoming. "What did Wally tell you?"

Lenny maneuvers me until my back is leaning against his front and he's massaging my temples. "Wally doesn't know much."

I moan at the feel of his fingers working their magic. He freezes for a second before continuing his ministrations.

"Wally, Chrissie's husband, doesn't know much?"

I guess Chrissie has kept my secrets. I'm not surprised. The woman isn't a tattletale. It's hard to be a tattletale and be a spy at the same time after all.

"What deal was William talking about?"

I groan and collapse against Lenny. He wraps his arms around me and draws me near. I close my eyes and soak in the comfort. I know it's wrong. I shouldn't take comfort from him when we can't be more than friends. It's wrong to lead him on this way.

But today of all days I could use some comfort. I knew William would lose his mind when I sent him the divorce papers. But I didn't expect him to track me down or inform me my parents expect me to return home.

Home? West Virginia isn't my home. My home is right here in Lenny's arms. Whoa, Lexi. Slow your roll. I pull away from Lenny. He resists for a second before letting me go with a sigh.

"We don't have to talk about this tonight."

I feign cleaning out my ear. "What did you say?"

"Smartass. Let's have a relaxing night. I'll order pizza and we'll watch a movie."

I narrow my eyes on him. "And you won't bring up William again?"

He crosses his heart. "Promise."

"Make pizza Chinese and I'm in."

"Deal."

I stand. "Can you call in our order? I'm going to shower."

He waggles his eyebrows. "And slip into something more comfortable."

"If you call flannel pajamas more comfortable, then yes I will."

He grins. "Your flannel pajamas are adorable."

I wag my finger at him. "No making fun of my flannel pj's. Wisconsin winters last for-freaking-ever."

I guess I've softened up living in the DC metro area. We got the occasional snowfall there, too, but nothing compares to a Wisconsin winter. The wind blowing off of Lake Michigan is colder than the wind off of Lake Baikal in Siberia. I'm exaggerating but not by much.

I enjoy a scalding hot but brief shower before dressing in my pajamas and joining Lenny on the sofa. He has a cold beer waiting for me on the coffee table. William never had a cold beer waiting for me after I showered. He expected me to wait on him hand and foot. The word jerk is not strong enough to describe William Harper.

I sigh. There's no comparison between Lenny and William and it's not fair to compare them anyway. One of them spent more than two decades of his life fighting for our freedoms while the other has spent his entire life abusing those freedoms.

I plop down next to Lenny and sip my beer.

"The food should be here soon. What do you want to watch?"

"Whatever you want is fine. As long as it's not serious. I have no interest in some award winning movie full of heart wrenching emotion." I feign gagging.

He chuckles. "Action adventure it is."

Before the film begins, the doorbell rings. I stand, but Lenny kisses my forehead. "I've got it. Sit. Relax."

Normally, I'd fight him. He's not in charge here. This is my place, after all. But I'm too emotionally worn out to argue with him right now. It's why I avoided telling him about William and my whole sordid history in the first place. It's not because I don't want to talk to him. Or, at least, it's not the only reason.

Lenny returns with several bags of food. My eyes widen. "Did you order the entire menu?"

"I wanted to give you the chance to pick and choose." He sets the bags down on the coffee table. "Let me grab some plates."

I stand. "I got it."

He points at me. "You're supposed to be relaxing. Sit down."

I should yell at him for ordering me around, but he's trying to take care of me. No one's taken care of me since I was five years old and learned how to light the wood-burning stove. Since then, I've had to fend for myself. I sound like I'm whining. I'm not. My parents— I shut off that train of thought and motion to the kitchen.

"Have at it."

I unpack the food. "Mmm… it all smells good. Bye-bye diet."

Lenny squeezes my shoulder. "You don't need to be on a diet, Whiskey."

People always assume because I'm lean, I don't need to diet. They're wrong. I'm lean because I diet. Not because I can eat whatever I want without consequences. After forty, no one can eat whatever they want without consequences.

We settle in with the food and some movie. Good thing there won't be a pop quiz after the movie's finished because I'm not following the plot. My mind is too busy whirling with the implications of what William told me today.

My parents expect me to return to West Virginia? William's going to fight the divorce? I should have known life was too good to be true.

"Enough," Lenny growls.

"What?" I scan the room, but nothing is amiss. "What's wrong?"

"What's wrong?" He taps my temple. "What's wrong is you're stuck in your head, worrying about everything."

I shrug. "It's hard not to. Things are going to get rough."

Lenny stretches out with his feet on the coffee table and lifts his arm. "Come here."

I frown. "Friends don't snuggle on the sofa together."

"We both know I'm more than a friend." I open my mouth, but he continues before I get the chance to speak. "No, don't deny it. Not tonight. Tomorrow, we can return to our dance but tonight I'm comforting you in any way I can."

I hate how he's right. I've been fighting us from the get-go because I've kind of been married the entire time, but I can no longer deny the truth. I care for Lenny, and I don't want him to stay in the friend zone. But the friend zone is where he has to stay until the issue with William is resolved.

Lenny's tired of waiting. He grasps my hand and tugs until I'm close enough for him to wrap his arm around me.

"Relax. No one is going to bother you now. You're safe here."

How I long for his words to be true. For now, I guess they are. I curl into his side and let myself relax. Just for tonight, I promise myself. Just for tonight.

Chapter 22

Your secrets are safe with me and all my friends.

I wake with a kink in my neck. Probably because my pillow is rock hard. Wait. What? My pillow isn't rock hard. I rub my hand over my pillow. Hold on. That's not a pillow.

Lenny grunts. "If I knew you'd fondle me upon waking, I would have fallen asleep on the sofa with you before this."

Oops! I jerk my hand away, but he catches it. "I'm not complaining."

Of course, he's not. He's been pushing for more than friendship since practically the minute I met him. I crane my neck to look up at him. He smiles down at me. His brown eyes shine, and I feel my belly warm at the tenderness in his gaze.

"Good morning, Whiskey." He kisses my hair, and I have to swallow a sigh at the feeling of his lips touching me.

I should berate him for kissing me and calling my Whiskey, but it's time I learn to accept Lenny is more than a friend. As much as the idea scares me.

"Why didn't you wake me?"

He chuckles. "I had you right where I want you – in my arms."

Stupid question.

"Do you want me to make you breakfast or do you want to go out?"

He's going to make me breakfast in my own home? It would be the second time he's made me breakfast which is two times more than any other man has done before – including William my 'husband'.

"What time is it? I should get to work."

The words are barely out of my mouth when the doorbell rings. I stand, but Lenny stops me.

"I got this."

"I can answer my own door."

"I know, but you don't have to when I'm here."

I scrunch my nose. "Are you trying to spoil me?"

"Damn straight. I'm going to spoil you until you're addicted to me taking care of you."

My mouth drops open. "You're serious?"

"As an M60 pointed at a Taliban terrorist."

The doorbell rings again before I have a chance to get my thoughts in order. He saunters to answer it and I can't help admiring his body as he walks. His body is all power in motion. He may be on the other side of fifty, but you wouldn't know it from the way he moves.

He peers through the peephole. "Your girl gang is here," he announces and opens the door.

"We brought food," Suzie says as she shoves her way past Lenny.

"Good. I'm starving," Phoebe says.

I stand. "What is everyone doing here? Shouldn't we be at the office soon?" I check my watch before I realize I'm still in my pajamas and thus not wearing a watch.

"*You Cheat, We Eat* is closed for a company retreat today," Hailey announces.

"Um, why?" I have a feeling her answer is not going to make me happy.

She rolls her eyes. "Duh. Because we're spending the day with you."

Suzie rubs her hands together. "Learning all about the mystery man." She points to Lenny. "You! Out! Now!"

Lenny chuckles as he walks over to me. He palms my neck and uses the hold to draw me near before resting his forehead against mine. "You okay spending the day with them, or do you need me to rescue you?"

My lips purse. "Rescue me? Do I look like the type of woman who needs rescuing?"

He sighs. "I couldn't fall for a woman who wasn't stubborn?"

Fall for? Does he mean? Before I have the chance to freak out, his lips touch mine in the briefest of kisses. "You have my number if you change your mind."

And with those words, he grabs his coat and strolls out of my house.

Suzie fans her face. "Whoa. Is it hot in here?"

Chrissie barges into the house. "Sorry I'm late. And are my eyes deceiving me or did I just see Lenny doing the walk of shame?"

The walk of shame? As if Lenny would ever be ashamed of anything he ever did. The man's middle name is confident.

Chrissie frowns when she notices my pajamas. "Not the walk of shame then."

"What's wrong with my pajamas?"

She snorts. "They don't exactly scream I got me some last night."

Phoebe squeals. "Does this mean I get to go lingerie shopping with Lexi?"

"Hear ye, hear ye." Hailey claps her hands. "I now bring this meeting to order."

"Meeting? I thought this was a company retreat?" I scan the room. "Speaking of which, Suzie and Chrissie no longer work at *You Cheat, We Eat.*"

"Ahem." Suzie points to herself. "I'm still an owner."

I cross my arms and focus my attention on Chrissie.

She smirks. "Actually, I'm a contractor at *You Cheat, We Eat.*"
"Explain."

"I passed my PI exam." She bows, and I roll my eyes. "And while I don't want to have an office at *You Cheat, We Eat,* Hailey and I—"

Suzie clears her throat.

"Excuse me. Hailey, Suzie, and I have come to an arrangement for me to use the administrative services of the firm."

I snort. "You mean I'm going to be doing all your invoicing and financial record keeping."

Chrissie grins. "Exactly!"

"Since everyone's caught up, let's move on to the first item on today's agenda." Hailey raises an eyebrow at me. "Who was the man yesterday? And what's the story?"

"Party foul. Those are two items," I point out.

Chrissie sighs. "Do you want me to tell them or are you going to?"

I gasp. "You're supposed to be my friend and keep my secrets."

She snorts. "We both know you're not surviving this day without telling the entire story."

The entire story? Nope. No way. No how. Never happening. Chrissie doesn't know the entire story and she never will. And neither will anyone else.

Phoebe leads me to the sofa. "Sit. Let me tell you a little story called Phoebe's husband wins the asshole award of the century."

This I've got to hear. Fifteen minutes later my mouth is gaping open as I stare at Phoebe. "You're joking." I knew her husband was in jail for kidnapping her, but I didn't realize he put the A in asshole.

"I didn't tell you my story to get your sympathy. I'm happy now." She rubs her baby bump with a look of bliss on her face. "I told you to show you you're not alone. Whoever the jerk from yesterday is and whatever he's done to you, we won't judge you."

Shit. I'd be a total bitch not to tell them the story now. And so, I do. I tell them the 'this is not a love story between Lexi Mullins and William Harper in the holler' leaving out one little tidbit. I rub my hand over my chest when the ache blossoms there. After all these years, the pain remains.

"Are you shitting me?" Hailey explodes when I finish.

"Nope."

"He's married to you but living with another woman? What a douche bag? No, he's too good for the word douche bag. After all, douche has a purpose. He has no purpose. We should kill him."

"Ryker already offered to hide the body."

Phoebe gasps. "My husband knew who he was and didn't tell me? I'm going to kill him."

She tries to get up from the sofa, but her belly makes it difficult. I help her to settle back down. "He doesn't know who William is to me, but he knows the guy's a jerk."

"Correction. He's a gobshite oxygen stealer scum of the earth shit face," Suzie clarifies.

I lift my hand and she slaps it. "True story."

"But why did he show up yesterday?" Chrissie asks.

"I served him with divorce papers in January. He wasn't amused."

"About freaking time," she mutters.

I sigh. "I didn't choose to stay married to him. It was part of the deal."

Suzie thrusts her hand in the air. "I call bullshit!"

Phoebe pats my arm. "I'm glad this will all be over for you soon."

"Um. Not over. He refuses to sign the papers."

"What?" Hailey screeches. "He has two children by another woman who – let me remind everyone in the class – is living with him. Who does he think he is? Not signing the papers?"

"May I point to Exhibit A once again. Aka the deal where our marriage brought the end to a decades long feud between the Mullins and the Harpers."

"Screw the deal," Chrissie snaps. "Divorce him anyway."

"I plan to. He's going to fight it, though."

She squeezes my hands. "Don't give in to him."

I rear back. "Why in the world would you think I'd give in to him?"

Does she think I'm some weak woman whose actions can be swayed by a man? I am not weak. Okay, yes. I agreed to this dumbass deal. But I was twenty-five at the time and backed into a corner. I didn't feel as if I had a choice. I know differently now, but the past is the past. I can't change it.

"I'm not going to give into him."

Suzie waggles her brows. "Especially not now you've got a silver fox of your own who wants to show you his bald-headed sailor."

"Lenny was a soldier, not a sailor."

"My comment stands."

"Whatever." I stand. "Someone promised me breakfast," I say to signal question and answer hour is over.

Chapter 23

Friends pick us up when we fall. And, if they can't pick us up, they lie down and listen for a while.

LENNY

I gave Lexi last night and today, but I'm done waiting. She's going to tell me what the deal is with William, *her husband.*

When she opens her door, I lift up the pizza and six-pack of beer. "Hungry?"

She motions me inside. "I've been grazing on food all day. There's some concern I may have turned into a cow."

I chuckle as I kiss her forehead. "You're the sexiest cow I've ever seen."

She points to her pajamas. The same pair she was wearing when I left this morning. "Because sexy cows always wear pj's with hearts on them."

"Naturally."

I set the pizza on the coffee table before heading to the kitchen to stow the beer in the refrigerator. "You want one?"

"Um." Her nose scrunches. "Are you going to interrogate me about William?"

"Interrogate? No. Demand you tell me everything? Yes."

She cocks her head to the side. "I'm confused. I'm not understanding what the difference is between interrogate and demand."

I smirk. "Instead of waterboarding, I'll bribe you with sexual favors."

Her eyes flare and her face flames. I take her reaction for the invitation it is. I leave the beers on the kitchen counter and stalk toward her. I cradle her face with my hands. "You like my idea?"

Her chest heaves as she pants, and her eyes dilate. She likes the idea all right. Good. She's finally on board with us moving our friendship on to another level. But first things first. I kiss the tip of her nose before stepping back. I gasp her hand, grab the beers, and lead her to the sofa.

"If this is the part where I confess all my deep, dark secrets, I veto."

I sip on my beer as I consider how to convince her to open up to me. Unlike what I just said, I'm not going to bribe her with sexual favors. It's too early in our relationship for those types of games. Besides, I don't want her to regret spilling her secrets. Honesty it is.

I set my beer on the coffee table before turning to her and squeezing her hands. "Listen, Whiskey. I haven't made a secret of how I feel about you. I want you to be mine and I want to be yours." I place a finger over her mouth when she opens it to speak.

"No. Don't fight me or give me some shit about us being friends right now. We both know it's a lie. Not only is there undeniable chemistry between us, but I genuinely like and admire you as a person. I want to know everything there is to know about you. I want to spend all my time with you. I can't stop thinking about you when you aren't near."

She snorts. "In other words, you're obsessed with me."

She's mocking me, but I don't deny it. "Hell yeah, I am. You're fucking perfect, Whiskey. Of course, I'm obsessed with you."

The smile falls from her face and her chin drops to her chest. "I'm far from perfect."

I cup her chin and force her head up, so I can look her into the eyes. "You're perfect to me."

"You lied. You're not bribing me with sexual favors, you're doing the whole 'guilting me into telling you everything' thing."

I waggle my eyebrows. "Is it working?"

"You're relentless. I should have listened closer when Chrissie told me how Wally captured her."

I drop my hands and she reaches for her beer. She downs half the bottle in one go. I decide it's time to give her some space to come to terms with how she's going to tell me her story.

She finishes off her beer before leaning back on the sofa and closing her eyes. "I grew up in West Virginia," she begins.

For the next thirty minutes, she talks. And as she talks, my anger grows. Her family is a bunch of assholes. They trapped her in a marriage she didn't want because she made a drunken mistake and slept with the enemy. I should plan a visit to West Virginia to show them exactly what I think of them. My brothers will join me. We'll make a road trip out of it.

"And there you have it," she concludes.

"Let me get this straight. You married William to settle the feud between your family and his?"

She nods.

"My question is – why did you agree to the deal in the first place?"

Her eyes flash with anger, and I know I'm on the right track. I knew she was holding back from me.

"I told you. I slept with William when I was drunk. When my parents found out, they pressured me into marrying him."

"I don't believe you."

Her eyes narrow on me. "How dare you? You weren't there. You don't know what happened."

"I know a brilliant girl, who worked her ass off to win a scholarship to Princeton and graduated with honors, would do anything to get away from her past and improve her future. What she wouldn't do is be shamed into marrying a man she doesn't even like by her parents."

"Doggone it, Lenny. I'm not telling you about her."

"Her?"

Her face pales as she shakes her head. "No. No. No."

I pick her up and place her on my lap so she's straddling me. I squeeze her neck to draw her near and place her forehead against mine.

"Whatever it is, whatever happened, you can tell me. There will be no judgment from me. And I promise I won't tell a soul anything you tell me in confidence."

"Not even your brothers?" she asks in a whisper.

"No one. Not even my priest at confession."

She forces a smile. "You're not Catholic and you don't go to confession."

"Then, it'll be easy for me to keep my word, won't it?"

"You also can't get mad and decide to kill William."

I growl. What the hell did he do to her?

"I can't promise you I won't get mad."

"In that case—"

I place a finger over her lips. "But I can promise I won't take my anger out on you. I will never take my anger out on you. Never."

She studies me for a long moment before puffing out a breath of air. "I married William because I was pregnant with his child. I know, I know, I could raise a child on my own, but there was no way William would let me leave the holler with his baby in my belly. He would have followed me to the ends of the earth and dragged me back by my hair. I didn't think I had a choice but to marry him."

Pregnant? Child? Lexi has a kid? Where is it? She. She said she. Where is she?

"You left your child to be raised by that man," I grumble.

She rears back. "How dare you? You said you wouldn't judge me. You promised!"

Shit. She's right. I'm being an ass. She tries to scramble off of my lap, but I don't let her go.

"I'm sorry. You shocked me. I misspoke."

She crosses her arms over her chest and leans back as far as possible while remaining perched on my lap.

"Apology not accepted."

I sigh. "I'm an ass. Are those the words you want to hear?"

"What I want is for you to not be an ass!"

I shrug. "I'm a man. I will be an ass on more occasions. And I trust you to point each and every occasion out to me."

"I will. You can bet on it."

"Okay, then. Where's your daughter?"

Her face crumples, and she curls in on herself. I maneuver her until she's cradled on my lap. "Tell me. Tell me quick and I promise we'll never speak of it again."

"She died." Her voice is so quiet I can barely hear her. "I went into labor early. William was out gallivanting, and I was home alone without any transportation. I called everyone I knew to try and find William, but when he doesn't want to be found, he won't be. When I started bleeding, I called an ambulance. They didn't arrive in time. I lost her and nearly bled out."

Tears stream down her face, and I rock her as she cries. I rub circles on her back and whisper nonsensical words to her until her tears slow. Once she's cried out, I wipe the wetness from her face.

"I'm sorry. I know it sounds trite, but I am truly sorry for your loss. I can't imagine how difficult it was for you. Thank you for telling me."

"The pizza must be cold by now," she says, and I know the discussion has been closed.

I can't bear to see Lexi this upset and have no problem moving the conversation on to a lighter subject. I set her on the sofa next to me and stand.

"I'll heat the pizza up in the microwave. You choose a movie to watch."

"I choose? What if I choose a romantic comedy?"

"Have at it."

I could give a shit what movie she chooses. Hasn't she figured it out by now? I'll give her anything she wants.

Chapter 24

There's nothing better than a friend, except a
friend with a flask.

LENNY TUGS ON MY hand to stop me before we can enter the hotel. "What's wrong? Is this outfit not okay?" I smooth a hand down my dress. I'm not exactly the kind of girl who dresses up for fun.

He tucks a strand of hair behind my ear. "You're beautiful."

"Then, what's wrong?" I rub a finger over the front of my teeth. "I don't have something stuck in my teeth, do I?"

"No, and before you come up with another reason to be nervous, there's not a single thing wrong with what you're wearing or your appearance. I wanted to check you're feeling okay is all."

"Feeling okay? Why wouldn't I be? I had three beers last night. I need to drink a heck of a lot more alcohol to feel hungover the next day." I point to myself. "Holler born and bred, remember?"

He sighs. "I wanted to check you're not upset because we're going to a baby shower."

Oh, yeah. I forgot there's someone else in the world who knows about baby Megan.

"I'm fine. It's not my first baby shower since Megan."

He cups my chin. "I know you're used to handling this all on your own, but those days are over. I care for you, and I will take your pulse over and over again to make sure you're doing alright. I will never let you enter a situation if it's going to upset you."

My belly flutters at his words. I haven't had anyone care for me in a long time. My parents weren't exactly what you would call warm and loving. Hugs and cuddles did not exist in our house. Skinned knee? There's the medicine cabinet. Lost a baby? You can always try again.

Except I couldn't try again. The doctors had to perform a hysterectomy to save my life. And even if I could, there was no way in hell I was trying with William. Except for the one drunken escapade, I never let him touch me again. I'm not a complete idiot.

"I can't believe Phoebe is having a co-ed baby shower," I say instead of responding to his sweetness. Something I'm not used to and don't know if I ever will be.

Lenny glances away and whistles. I slap his chest. "What did you do?"

"I may have talked to Ryker about the idea of having a co-ed baby shower. He was all for it."

Of course, he was. Ryker can't stand for Phoebe to be out of his sight. Considering the story she told me about her ex-husband, I can understand why.

"I'm not in danger," I repeat for the millionth time.

"Danger isn't always physical."

Damn it. There goes my stomach melting again at his words. "Stop being sweet!"

"Get used to it." He tugs on my hand. "Come on. I've never been to a baby shower before."

When we enter the room Phoebe reserved for her shower, I can't help a giggle from escaping. It's all pink and frilly. There are pink roses everywhere. Even the cups and plates have pink roses on them. This is not a place most men would enter without being forced.

Speaking of men, they're congregated around a bar at the far corner. Except for Ryker, whose gaze is focused on his wife, they're fidgeting and looking around like they have no idea how they got here.

"Huh. I didn't expect there to be a full bar here."

"There wasn't," Suzie explains. "Phoebe added it when Ryker insisted this event would be co-ed. Thanks a lot for that, by the way."

I widen my eyes. "What? It's not my fault."

"Don't pretend we don't know this guy," she points at Lenny, "went all protective on your ass since your ex is still loitering around town."

Grayson clears his throat. "We talked about this."

She bats her eyelashes at him. "What did we talk about?"

He sighs. "I need to hydrate."

"Yes, yes, you do, my glorious stud muffin."

"You're a nut, Munchkin." He kisses her hair before strolling off to the bar.

Lenny squeezes my hand. "Are you going to be okay alone?"

Suzie shoves her way between us. "You. Go." She indicates the bar with a sweep of her hand. "It's girl talk time."

He grunts before kissing the tip of my nose and following Grayson.

"Good. They're gone. Now tell Auntie Suzie the truth. Have you roasted Willy's broomstick yet?"

"Roasted his broomstick? You sure know how to make sex sound appealing. Not."

"Sex? Who's had sex?" Val asks as she joins us. "Please tell me it's Lexi and Lenny."

I cock my eyebrow. "Don't you have July 4th?"

She waves away my question. "Who cares about winning the bet? I want to see you all loved up. Especially after I found out about that jerk William. I'm telling you marriage is bad."

How does Val know about William? She wasn't at the 'company retreat' when I confessed all my deep dark secrets. I frown at the women who are now surrounding me. "Is there anyone who doesn't know about William?"

"Darling, I know and I'm always the last to hear," Mary Ann says. "By the way, why am I always the last to hear?"

Val hip checks her. "Maybe because you work sixty hours a week and spend all your free time playing hide your wand in the chamber of secrets with Sid."

Suzie slaps Val's hand. "Good one."

Mary Ann sighs. "Sid's wand is pretty magical."

Phoebe feigns gagging. "I don't want to hear about my uncles having sex."

Hailey shrugs. "I don't mind." She smirks as she turns to Faith. "Feel free to share with the class."

I need to stop this before it gets out of hand. Today is Phoebe's day. She should be able to enjoy it however she wants. Apparently, she wants to sit around and drink tea. Fine. I can do this. I clap my hands to get everyone's attention.

"Why don't we take our seats. Phoebe, I assume the throne is for you?" I indicate the chair in the middle of one of the tables with balloons floating above it.

"I hope there's lots of food. Baby Grayson's hungry," Suzie says before discarding her coat.

I freeze when I see her outfit. "What are you wearing?"

Her brow scrunches in confusion. "What do you mean?" She indicates her outfit. "The invitation said to dress for a tea party."

"And you choose to wear …" I wave my hand around as I don't know how to describe her outfit.

"Are you the mad hatter?" Val asks.

"Yes!" Suzie shouts. "Thank goodness someone knows how to read a book."

Phoebe sighs. "I never thought I needed to specify what tea party attire is on the invitation," she mumbles.

Suzie sticks out a foot. "What? This is tea party attire."

Her legs are covered in green and yellow striped tights. Her pencil skirt features a pattern of black diamonds over which she's wearing a short-sleeve green jacket with puffy sleeves and a floppy, yellow bowtie.

"How did you even get your skirt over your belly?"

"It's stretch. And before you ask, Grayson had to help me with the tights. Don't worry. I rewarded him." She winks.

"Poor Grayson is going to need a vacation by the time she gives birth," Hailey mumbles into my ear.

I take Phoebe's elbow and lead her to her chair.

"My queen," I bow to her once she's seated.

"See?" Suzie says as she plops down next to Phoebe. "I needed to wear the mad hatter outfit because Phoebe is the Queen of Hearts."

So much for being the only one who can read. "The Queen of Hearts wasn't at the tea party."

Suzie flicks her hand. "Whatever."

I find an empty chair across the table and down from Suzie. I love the woman, but she can be a bit much at times. Chrissie rushes inside and sits down next to me.

"Why are you late?"

Wally strolls in and ambles through the room to the bar where the other men are congregating. The smile on his face stretches from ear to ear.

"Never mind."

A team of servers arrive and begin placing three tiered stands stuffed with sandwiches on the table as well as pots filled with water and trays of various types of tea. I notice the table behind us for the men remains empty.

"They're having burgers and fries," Phoebe explains.

My brow wrinkles. "From these dainty plates?" I pick up the plate decorated with flowers and edged with gold.

She shrugs. "I didn't exactly have much time to add an additional eight guests to the party."

"I'm sorry. I didn't—"

She holds up a hand. "No, I'm sorry. I channeled my mother there for a minute." She does an exaggerated shiver. "I don't care about the extra guests. Besides, Ryker claimed he was going to crash the party anyway. At least this way, he won't be standing on his own in the corner scaring all the wait staff away," she says before turning away to answer a question from Suzie about whether tea is good for pregnant women.

Chrissie leans close to whisper, "Speaking of men scaring people away." She tilts her head toward Lenny who is indeed standing at the edge of the group with his arms crossed over his chest and glaring at anyone who enters the room.

"Someone's gone into overprotective mode," I mutter.

"I guess you finally told him about the baby."

My eyes widen and my mouth falls open. "You know about her?"

She rolls her eyes. "Duh. What kind of spy would I be if I didn't?"

"You didn't …"

She pats my arm. "Of course not. I haven't told a soul including Wally." My shoulders deflate. Phew. "But if you ever want to talk, I'm here."

"Thank you."

"There's no reason to thank me. We're friends."

I started this week believing there was no one to share my grief with and now I have two people who are standing by me. Maybe I should have shared with Chrissie before this?

Chapter 25

Friends comfort you with kindness. Brothers
from different mothers comfort you with
promises of revenge.

LENNY

"And?"

At Wally's question, I drag my gaze away from Lexi to ask him, "And what?"

"What are you going to do about Lexi's husband?"

I can't help but growl when I hear the word *husband*. William is no husband to Lexi. He never was. I'd be hard pressed to call him a man after what he did.

"He is not her husband," I grumble.

"Okay. I can concede your point, but my question stands. What are you going to do?"

"I'm thinking a shallow grave is too good for him." He doesn't deserve a grave considering he was out chasing tail while Lexi lay at home losing her baby and bleeding out.

"I'm in," Sid says as he joins us.

"This is not a joke," I tell him. I love my brother, but he gets bored way too easily and gets off on dangerous missions. He needs to find a hobby that doesn't involve playing poker or pool at Max's bar.

"What are we going to do? Torture him?" Max asks, and I glare at him.

"*We* are not doing anything."

Wally crosses his arms over his chest. "What are *you* going to do, brother?"

"I don't know. It's up to Lexi."

I've watched as all of my brothers fell in love over the past year, and I've watched them all make the same mistake – treat the woman they love as if she can't handle things herself. I'm not making the same mistake.

Sid sighs. "Damn. Just when things were starting to get exciting again."

Max punches his shoulder. "Suzie and Phoebe are having kids soon. That ought to be enough excitement for you."

He wrinkles his nose. "Poopy diapers aren't exactly dangerous."

Max barks out a laugh. "You've obviously never changed a poopy diaper."

I ignore them in favor of watching Ryker approach his wife. He bends down and whispers in her ear. She frowns but nods. I guess the party's over. Time to claim Lexi.

"You ready?"

Lexi giggles. "Why? Are you going to do a jig on top of the table?"

I help her stand and draw her near. "I didn't think there was any alcohol at this party."

She rolls her eyes. "You really don't know me well, do you?"

"She brought her flask of moonshine," Chrissie says in a voice I'm sure she thinks is a whisper but is the volume of a shout.

"I'm going to have to start patting you down for contraband before we leave the house."

She winks. "You'll use any excuse to get your hands on me, won't you?"

"Damn straight I will," I growl into her ear and smile as goosebumps appear.

She tilts her head in invitation, but a baby shower is not the place to show her how much I want to taste her skin.

"Let's get you home." I place a hand on her lower back and lead her out of the room.

She twists in my hold. "Bye, Chrissie! You're the best!"

Chrissie waves. "You're my girl, Lexi. My girl." She makes a heart shape with her hands, which causes her to lose her balance. Wally chuckles as he catches her before she can fall.

I lead Lexi out of the hotel. She skips as we head toward the parking garage.

"I thought moonshine didn't affect you."

She frowns at me. "It's not the moonshine. I'm happy." She throws out her arms before twirling in a circle. "Check out the sky. Isn't it gorgeous?"

Not exactly how I'd describe the sky right now. It's nearly pitch black despite it being the middle of the afternoon as a thunderstorm is on its way.

Lexi screeches to a halt when she sees the SUV. "You know if I hadn't felt how big your manhood is against my stomach, I'd think you're trying to compensate for little man's disease with this vehicle."

In case I don't know what she means with 'little man's disease' she indicates with her thumb and forefinger.

"You're not this small." She opens her arms wide. "More like this big."

"I don't think any man is that big. How would it fit?"

She taps her chin as she considers the question. "You're right. The poor woman. Talk about pain. Although, women can handle pain. We are the stronger gender after all."

"Of course, you are," I murmur.

"We can literally shoot watermelons out of us. No man can do anything nearly as impressive with his penis."

I wrap an arm around her middle and pull her flush with me. "Now, now, Whiskey. There are plenty of impressive things I can do with mine."

"Let me guess. You can demonstrate." She bursts into giggles.

"I'll demonstrate all day and all night."

Her breasts strain against me as she fights to catch her breath. "All day and all night?"

"One word, babe. Stamina."

She sighs and pushes away from me. "Promises. Promises."

I open the passenger door of the SUV and hold out my hand to her. She doesn't accept it. Of course, not. This woman is stubborn about the silliest things. Instead, she takes a flying leap at the door and jumps into the seat.

"Tada!" She bows as if she performed some kind of miraculous feat making me wonder exactly how much moonshine she drank.

I draw the seatbelt across her body, kiss her forehead, and shut the door.

Once we're driving toward her house, I decide to broach the subject of her ex with her. And I do mean her ex. He's not her current husband no matter what some stupid piece of paper says.

I feign a casualness I don't feel and ask, "Have you thought about what you're going to do next about William?"

She grunts as she lays her head against the backrest and closes her eyes. "What can I do? He won't sign the divorce papers, and I'm not giving up. I don't think I have any other option except to hire an attorney and sue him for divorce. Lord knows I've got the grounds to ask for one."

"How will your family respond?"

"They're going to lose their doggone minds. Based on the number of times they've called since I served William the divorce papers, they're already losing their minds. I expect the entire clan to show up at my house any day now."

She doesn't sound happy to have her family invade. Such a shame. She should be excited for her family to visit. But they haven't been much of a family to her considering the deal they forced her to make.

"How would you feel if I talked to William?"

Her eyes fly open. "You want to talk to William?"

"Man to man." Although I don't consider him a man, something I plan to make perfectly obvious when we speak.

"Why are you asking me?"

"Because it's your business, not mine."

Her nose scrunches. "Really? You want to be more than friends with me, but my having a husband is *my* business?"

My heart squeezes and my belly warms at her words. Finally! Lexi is finally on the path to us being more than 'just' friends. Took her long enough.

"To be perfectly clear, you won't be mad if I go talk to William without you?"

"Do you need me to spell it out for you?" She lifts her right hand. "I, Alexis Mullins, will not give you the silent treatment or otherwise punish you should you decide to have a 'talk' with William Harper." She lowers her hand. "You got me?"

I nod. Does she realize she's handing me the key to open the gate to life beyond the friend zone? If she doesn't know, I'm not telling her. I'm bursting through the gate and destroying it in my wake.

"But…"

Crap. Here it comes.

"If you happen to…" she clears her throat, "end up harming William in any way, I am not helping you bury the body – call Ryker, he'll help – and I'm not visiting you in the slammer."

"I'm offended. I'd never get caught." There's more than one reason I've stayed close friends with Wally all these years.

"As long as we're on the same page."

"We are."

"Of the same book," she clarifies.

"I got you. You do not help bury bodies."

"Shoveling is hell on my nails and I just had a manicure."

"And you won't visit me in the slammer."

"Although, I will hold up a sign outside the courthouse while your trial is occurring that says 'Free Willy'."

"Since my name is Lenny, I'm not sure how that helps."

She shrugs. "I never claimed to be helpful."

"You're a nut."

"Crunchy and delicious is my game. Nut is my name!"

"Exactly how much moonshine did you drink?"

She removes a flask from her hip and holds it upside down. "All gone, although Chrissie helped. Not Hailey, though. She can't handle the shine."

I want to tell her she can't handle the shine either, but she's being hilarious. If this is how she acts after drinking a flask of moonshine, I need to stock up because a relaxed and happy Lexi is a Lexi I want to be around every minute of every day.

Chapter 26

Good friends don't let you do stupid things alone.

LENNY

I waste no time driving to William's hotel after I drop Lexi off at her house. I don't need to research where he's staying. I know exactly where he is. I've been keeping an eye on him since he showed up on Wednesday. I know he hasn't returned home yet. I assume he thinks he can pressure Lexi into giving in. He doesn't know a thing about my woman if he thinks he has a chance in hell of pressuring her to get his way.

I wait at the entrance of the hotel until Wally, Sid, Max, and Barney exit Wally's truck and join me.

I cross my arms over my chest. "What are all of you doing here?"

"We're not letting you go into an unknown situation without backup, brother," Wally answers.

I cock an eyebrow. "Unknown situation? I'm here to have a conversation with Lexi's husband. Nothing more."

Sid makes a fist. "I know what kind of conversation I'm voting for."

"I promised Lexi I wouldn't beat him up."

Max wrinkles his brow. "Lexi doesn't seem like the type of woman who'd care if he got a bit roughed up."

I shrug. She doesn't care. Or at least she says she doesn't. I don't want to chance her changing her mind and then I'm the thug who used brute force on her husband.

Barney opens his arms wide. "What do you call a tree that's afraid to fight?"

Wally elbows him. "Come on. William's in room 604."

I don't bother asking how he knows which room William's in. I learned long ago to accept his mysterious ways of knowing everything. Which made Chrissie holding out on him and not telling him about her past tons of fun to watch unfold.

While we ride the elevator to the sixth floor and stroll down the corridor toward room 604, I make peace with my brothers' involvement. I should have known better than to think I'd get the chance to confront William on my own. Don't get me wrong. I love my brothers, but this is a conversation I wanted to have man to man. Not man to many.

I pound on the door and William shouts, "Hold your dog-gone horses."

The door swings open, and his eyes widen as he takes in me and my entourage.

"What are all y'all doing here? Did something happen to Lexi?"

His concern flips a switch in me, and I snap. I wrap a hand around his neck while I shove him inside the room. I hear the door close behind me and know my brothers have my six.

"Do not pretend to care about what happens to Lexi," I scowl at William.

His eyes widen, although his response may be a result of a lack of oxygen to his brain. I loosen my hold on his neck enough for him to be able to gasp for breath. My hold is still uncomfortable as hell, but he won't die.

"She told ya?"

"Why wouldn't she tell me?"

"She doesn't tell anyone."

"How the hell would you know? You're not a part of her life."

"I'm her husband," he grits out.

Fuck ensuring my hold doesn't suffocate him to death. I tighten my hold and he scratches at my hands in an effort for me to release him. I ignore his pathetic attempts.

"You're only her husband because you tricked a poor pregnant girl into thinking she had no choice but to marry you."

His hands halt their attempt to make me release him. "She really did tell y'all everything."

Why does this asshat doubt Lexi's connection with me? I ignore his comment and get to the reason for this visit.

"This is what's going to happen." I use my hold on his neck to shake his body. "Are you listening?" He nods and I continue. "You're going to sign the divorce papers and then you're going to walk away and go back home and never bother Lexi again."

"I can't."

My hand squeezes his neck until his face is bright red.

"Why not?"

When he doesn't answer, I squeeze harder.

"Um, brother?" Sid calls out. "I think you need to loosen your hold if you want him to answer verbally."

I glare at William for a second before loosening my hold a fraction. "Do you understand my instructions?"

"I can't," he repeats.

"Is this when we beat the shit out of him?" Wally asks.

"Finally! I thought we'd never get to the good stuff," Barney adds.

"I call dibs on his ribs," Sid yells. "Hey. That rhymed. I'm a poet and I didn't even know it."

Where William's face was bright red before, it's now pale. I can't help myself from smiling. There's no better feeling than knowing my brothers always have my back.

"Why can't you?" I ask William. "You're living with another woman and her children who also happen to be your children."

"If I divorce Lexi, the feud between our kin will start up again."

"And this is Lexi's problem, why?"

"She's a Mullins."

Does he think saying her last name out loud is some kind of excuse? It's not. Besides, if I have anything to do with it, her last name won't be Mullins for long. Lexi Walker has a nice ring to it. Although, knowing my stubborn girl, she won't want to take my name.

From the corner of my eye, I notice Barney raise his hand. "I don't understand. Can someone explain to the class why she has to stay married to this lying, cheating piece of scum because her last name is Mullins? We can always run her down to the courthouse and have her change her legal name."

Max smirks at me. "I'm sure Lenny already has a plan to change her last name."

"Lexi can have her piece on the side, but I ain't giving her no divorce."

"Give her a divorce? Do you honestly think you have a say in the matter?" I shake my head. "Poor little man, he has no idea."

"Wally, back pocket."

Lexi handed me an extra set of divorce papers before I left her house. This asshat is going to sign them.

"Barney, you still a notary?"

"Brought my stamp with me for this very occasion."

"I ain't signing those. And y'all can't make me!"

Barney moans. "I hate when the crying starts. It's boring."

"I ain't crying!"

"Can we gag him?" Max asks.

I use my hold on William's neck to guide him to a chair I force him into. The second my hand leaves his neck he rubs it.

"I'm fixin' to call the cops on y'all."

I call his bluff and remove my phone from my back pocket. "Here. Go ahead."

He frowns but makes no move to accept the phone. I return it to my pocket.

"Listen, William. Here's the thing. You are going to divorce, Lexi. You can drag it out for a year by contesting it, but the divorce is going to happen. No judge will refuse to grant Lexi a divorce considering your lying, cheating ways."

"Y'all ain't got no idea. Y'all ain't from the holler. Y'all don't know what a judge back home will do."

I cross my arms over my chest and glare down at him. "Do you honestly think this divorce will be adjudicated in the holler? Boy, you're dumber than I thought, and I already thought you were pretty fucking dumb."

"I ain't letting her serve those dang papers. I can hide from a processor server until the cows come home."

I sigh. I bet he thinks he can.

I hand him a pen. "Sign the damn papers."

"Or what? All y'all gonna beat the shit out of me? Real original."

"For once in your life, be a man."

He sticks out his chin. "I am a man."

"No man leaves his pregnant wife home alone without any transportation, so he can chase some tail."

He gulps. "It ain't my fault. She turned into a cold bitch after we got married."

I clench my teeth as my hands fist. Before I can smash my fist into his face, Wally grabs me and drags me away. "Not worth it, brother."

"But it'd feel fucking fantastic."

"I'm sure it would. But remember the objective."

I still at his words. Wally was our team leader on too many missions to count. He knows how to make sure we focus to get the job done. Focus, Lenny. Focus.

I nod to indicate I've got myself under control and Wally releases me. I slam my fist down on the desk.

"Lexi is not a cold bitch. You tricked her into your bed when she was drunk and vulnerable and stole her innocence. Another thing a real man doesn't do. A woman is not a mountain to be conquered."

"I'm sick and tired of y'all saying I'm not a man."

I pat him on top of his head. "Then, man up and sign the damn papers. Give Lexi this one thing. She's never asked you for anything before. And you owe her."

"I—"

Max growls. "If the next words out of your mouth are I don't owe Lexi, I'm not going to hold these men back when they beat the daylights out of you."

William's shoulders hunch and he huffs out a breath of air. "Fine. I'll sign. But this ain't over. Her kin ain't gonna be okay with our divorce."

"One hurdle at a time."

I point to the sticky tabs indicating where William should sign. Once he's signed everywhere necessary, Wally does his notary thing.

"I'll have her lawyer file these in the morning," I say as I stick the papers into my pocket.

"Make sure you're gone in the morning, or I won't hold my brothers back next time," Wally orders as we leave.

I wait until we're outside before I address my brothers. "You can't tell your wives about the baby. Lexi doesn't want anyone knowing."

"No need to ask, brother. No need to ask." Max clamps a hand on my shoulder. "You okay? Or you want to hit the gym?"

"I'm good. I need to get back to Lexi."

Max squeezes my shoulder and stares into my eyes for a second before nodding.

I waste no time heading to my vehicle. I can't wait to see the expression on Lexi's face when she realizes she's free of William.

Chapter 27

Friends give you a shoulder to cry on. Best friends are ready with a shovel to hurt the person who made you cry.

"Go away!" I yell when the doorbell rings.

I'm too comfortable to move. I ditched my 'dress appropriate for a tea party' and threw on some sweats the minute Lenny dropped me off. I'm now under a blanket on the sofa while watching some home renovation show on television.

Don't judge. Home renovations shows are the bomb. Who doesn't love a 'big reveal' where the owners get everything they ever wanted?

"It's Lenny!"

"Don't care. I'm not moving until my bladder explodes."

Doggone it. I had to say the word bladder. Now, I have to pee. I grunt before throwing the blanket off of me. After I use the facilities, I return to the living room to find Lenny standing in the open doorway. Figures, he wouldn't wait.

"Miss me?" I bat my lashes at him. "Can't live without me?"

"Can't and don't want to," he says before he pulls me near, and his lips smash down on mine.

I gasp and he seizes the opportunity to shove his tongue in my mouth. This is no 'getting to know you' kiss. This kiss is one-hundred percent claiming. I want to fight him. He can't claim me. I'm not ready yet. Not to mention the whole 'William'-situation. But the feel of his tongue gliding into my mouth causes me to forget why I'm fighting us being together, and I melt into him.

Lenny wrenches his lips from mine and leans his forehead against mine while he gasps for breath. "I love it when you let go, Whiskey."

I stick out my button lip. "Then, why'd you stop?"

"One, we have things to discuss. And, two, your door's standing wide open. I'm not giving the neighbors a show for free."

"But you'd give them a show for a fee?"

He smirks. "If that's what you want."

Dang him. He called my bluff. I motion him inside. "Get your butt in here then, Mr. Paid Exhibitionist."

I grab two beers from the refrigerator. "You said we have things to discuss. What?"

"You remember our conversation in the car on the way home from the baby shower?"

I roll my eyes. "Of course, I do. It was less than two hours ago. I'm not the senile one in this relationship, old man."

I offer him a beer, but he ignores it to palm my neck and drag me near. "I'll show you who's an old man."

I do an exaggerated sigh. "You keep on making all these promises, but I have yet to see any execution. I'm beginning to think you're all talk."

"Speaking of talk. We need to talk."

I groan. "Ugh. No good has ever come from a conversation starting with the words 'we need to talk.'"

He grins. "I might surprise you."

We settle on the sofa with our beers. Lenny sips from his beer but doesn't say a word.

"I thought you wanted to talk."

He frowns. "I messed up. I should have bought roses or champagne or something."

"Roses and champagne? You better not be planning to propose Lenny Walker."

A vision of Lenny down on one knee with a diamond ring in his hand pops into my head and my heart races at the vision. I've always wanted one of those out of control proposals. Probably because the first and only proposal I ever got was William grunting before saying 'I guess we're getting married'.

He winks. "Trust me. When I propose, it's going to surprise the hell out of you."

When? He can't be serious. We barely know each other. Is he forgetting I'm not free to marry someone else?

"But we haven't even had sex yet," are the idiotic words that leave my mouth.

He smirks. "I'll add 'sex with Lexi' to my to-do list."

My belly warms and tingles spread down my body to my core. "You need to put sex on your to-do list, or you'll forget? I guess you proved who the senile one is in this relationship."

Yes, I said relationship. There's no sense denying it any longer. And I'm done fighting Lenny smashing at my walls. I can't win against his battering ram and, frankly, I don't want to. He knows all my secrets now anyway.

"Smart ass. I'm fifty-seven, not ninety-seven."

"What did you want to discuss?"

He finishes his beer and sets it on the coffee table before leaning forward and removing a set of papers from his back pocket. "These are for you."

I feel my nose scrunch. "What are…"

My voice trails off when I notice the documents are the same bunch I handed him before he left this afternoon. "Are these …"

I flip through the pages. Holy balls! William signed the divorce papers!

I pretend to study the pages. "I don't see any blood splatter."

"No blood was shed."

I cock an eyebrow. "Not even a broken nose?"

"I didn't want you to have to break your promise to me to visit me in prison, and you know William is the type of man to go whining to the police about a little thing like a broken nose."

As if Lenny would have kept it to a broken nose.

"How did you convince him to sign?"

He shrugs. "He needed a little persuading is all."

"And you persuaded him?"

"Me and my brothers."

I freeze. "Your brothers? Do they… Did you…" I rub a hand against my chest as pain slashes through me at the idea of his brothers knowing about Megan. About how I failed my baby girl.

Lenny scowls, and the next thing I know I'm straddling him. "You did not fail Megan."

A tear escapes, and he wipes it away.

"I didn't say I did."

"But you were thinking it and I'm not letting anyone say bad things about my woman. Not even my woman can say bad things about herself."

"But I should have known I was in labor before my water broke. I should have called someone to come pick me up and take me to the hospital sooner."

He pinches my lips shut. "No. You are not blaming yourself. You are not to blame. Megan was weeks early. How could you have possibly known you were in labor?"

I drop my gaze. I can't look into his sincere eyes. He doesn't know. He wasn't there. His hands move to cradle my face.

"You are not to blame." I squeeze my eyes shut. "Imagine the same thing had happened to Chrissie? Would you blame her for hurting her child?"

My eyes fly open, and I scoff. "Of course not."

"Then, Whiskey, you can't blame yourself."

I shake my head. "No. I can't forgive myself for what happened."

"You can't forgive yourself because there's nothing to forgive. Repeat after me. I am not at fault."

I clamp my lips shut. I can't say those words.

"What did the doctors say?"

"What do they know?" I hiss.

He raises an eyebrow. "Do you hear yourself?"

I slump against him. "It's just… I miss her. There's this hole in my heart with her name on it and no matter what I do the hole never gets any smaller."

He tucks a strand of my hair behind my ear. "And it shouldn't. But if you stop blaming yourself for Megan's death, maybe the pain will lessen. I'm not saying it will stop hurting completely, but maybe if you open up your heart and talk to your friends about Megan, the pain will be more bearable."

I grunt. "Chrissie said the same thing."

Surprise flares in his eyes "You talked to Chrissie about Megan?"

"No. The spy figured it out all on her own." Between her and Wally, I doubt any of us will be able to keep a secret very long. Do they spend all of their time running checks on their friends or what?

"Good. I'm glad you have a friend you can talk to Megan about. In fact, maybe it's an idea to join a support group. It might help to talk to other women who've experienced the same tragedy as you."

I grunt. I've never dared attend a support group before because I didn't want anyone I know to find out about Megan. No, that's not right. I didn't want anyone to know how I failed my baby girl.

I inhale a deep breath and let all my guilt about Megan go – for now. It'll be back tomorrow, but maybe Lenny's right, maybe I should talk to someone who's experienced what I have before.

"Okay, I'll look into support groups."

Lenny kisses my forehead. "Now, if our first agenda item is complete, I believe we have a second agenda item to attend to."

When I note the fire in his eyes, my entire body warms. "I think you're on to something, Mr. Walker."

The divorce papers are signed. There's no reason to deny myself what I want any longer.

Chapter 28

We're friends now. When do the benefits kick in?

LENNY

I stand with Lexi in my arms and stalk toward the bedroom. She tightens her legs around me, and my cock stands to attention.

"Where are we going? That's a perfectly good couch, you know."

"The first time I sink inside you will not be on a couch. I want to lay you out on the bed and take my time exploring your body."

She shivers at my words. "Okay," she murmurs before her tongue peeks out and she licks a path from my ear down my neck to my shoulder where she nips at me. My cock twitches at the feel of her teeth.

"You're a bad girl," I growl at her.

She winks at me. "Y'all ain't seen nothin' yet."

Shit. My stamina doesn't stand a chance against her West Virginian drawl. I clear my throat and wrestle my desire to throw her on the bed under control. "Promises. Promises."

Her hand dives into my jeans and she squeezes my ass. Screw finding the bed.

"You're a vixen, Whiskey," I grumble before I twirl around and press her against the wall next to the bed. My mouth slams down on hers. Any thought of gentle goes out the window as I plunder her mouth. Our tongues duel for dominance and our teeth clash.

Lexi uses her hold on my ass to drag me near and I thrust my hard length against her core. She moans and rips her mouth from mine to arch against me. The muscles in her neck strain as her head flies backward to hit the wall.

I run my teeth along the cords of her neck and goosebumps appear in my wake. I sink my teeth into the flesh between her neck and shoulder, and she rewards me with a long moan while her fingernails dig into my skin.

I pull down her t-shirt to reveal her naked flesh. "You're not wearing a bra."

She gazes down at me with eyes glossy from desire and lips swollen from my kisses. I've never seen such a beautiful sight. She bites her bottom lip and winks at me. "Easy access."

"I'm going to have to change my nickname for you from Whiskey to Vixen."

"I don't care what you call me as long as you get to work."

I grind my cock into her. "Do you mean like this?"

She moans. "Yes."

I freeze, and her head snaps forward to glare at me. I hold her gaze as I move to nip at the flesh of her breast. "Or do you mean like this?"

"What's wrong, old man? You can't do both at once?"

Now, she's asking for it. I make sure my hold on her is secure before I whirl around with her in my arms and throw her onto the bed. She giggles as she bounces on the mattress. I pounce on her making sure to keep the majority of my weight off of her, so I don't crush her.

"You think it's funny to tease me about my age?"

She licks her lips. "Damn straight."

"Let's see how funny you think this is."

I whip her t-shirt off of her, but in a move she doesn't see coming, I use the material to tie her wrists to her headboard. I trail a finger down her chest between her heaving breasts.

"You're at my mercy now."

"I'm so scared," she mocks as she arches her back in a clear invitation.

I soothe my hands over her stomach, making sure to avoid her breasts. When her nipples harden in response, I skim circles around the smooth skin underneath her breasts with my finger. Her skin breaks out in goosebumps, and she rubs her legs together.

I wag my finger at her. "Nuh-uh. No finding relief on your own."

I wrench her legs apart until I can nestle my hips between her thighs. She immediately wraps her legs around me and rubs herself against my cock.

I growl. "What did I say?"

She rolls her eyes. "You're too slow."

I lift an eyebrow. "Impatient, are we?"

She grunts. "Stop teasing."

She's asking for it now. I grasp the sides of her sweatpants and pull them down her legs. I groan when I realize she's not wearing any panties.

"Do you run around without a bra and panties on all the time?"

"Sitting at home watching television is hardly running around." Her words are a tease, but she's panting.

She lifts her hips, offering herself to me. It's an invitation I can hardly refuse. My hands skim up her thighs, pushing them apart as I go. I lower myself until my shoulders are cradled between her thighs, and she balances her feet on my shoulders.

I stare into her eyes as I lick her thigh until I reach her core. Her eyes close and her head falls back. I stop. "No. Watch me."

She tilts her chin forward and blinks her eyes open. "Are we going to lay here staring into each other's eyes or are you going to do something, old man?"

I glide my nose along the length of her seam before my tongue joins the party. This time when her eyes fall closed, I don't complain. I lick a circle around her clit before pressing my tongue against the hard nub. Her responding moan causes my cock to twitch.

Time to speed things up before my cock decides to break my promise of having stamina. I plunge a finger into her wetness and her hips nearly buck me off of her. I add another finger and while my fingers plunge in and out of her, I continue to torture her clit with my tongue.

It's not long before she's chanting my name, "Lenny, Lenny, Lenny."

I pause, and her chin drops to her chest as her eyes fly open. "Why did you stop?"

"I want you to scream my name when you come."

She rolls her eyes. "What is this? Some corny romance novel? I don't scream when I come."

"We'll see about that," I say before I plunge my tongue into her wetness while pinching her clit.

She tightens around my tongue as she shouts, "Yes, Lenny!"

Satisfaction fills my chest at her shout. I continue to plunge my tongue in and out of her as she rides out her orgasm. I only stop when she collapses on the bed. I kiss her thigh before crawling up her body. Her legs clamp around me to halt my movements.

"You're wearing too many clothes."

"You want me naked, Whiskey?" I wink as I stand from the bed. "Naked is what you get."

I whip off my t-shirt. I smirk when her eyes flare as she studies my chest. I work hard to maintain my body, and it shows. I skim my hands down my chest before my fingers find my belt buckle. She licks her lips as I undo the buckle and unsnap my jeans. I toe off my boots while I shove my jeans down my legs.

"You forgot something." She nods to my underwear.

My cock is hard and straining against the waistband. I push the material out of the way and my cock springs free.

"And there you have it, folks. Proof the large vehicle is not a result of small man's syndrome."

I fist my cock. "Damn straight, it isn't."

"Now come over here and show me you know how to use it."

I lift an eyebrow. "After you screamed my name, you still need proof I know how to use this?" I pump my hand up and down a few times.

"I didn't scream your name."

My Lexi. Always so damn stubborn. But if she wants me to prove I know how to use my cock to get her off, I'm up for the challenge.

I crawl onto the bed until our bodies are perfectly aligned. I can feel her breasts straining against my chest. She rubs them against my chest as her mouth drops open. It's an invitation I can't refuse. My lips meet hers and my tongue immediately dives in.

I'm enjoying her taste of lavender and springtime when she flips us until she's on top. I open my eyes to see her straddling me with a smirk on her face.

"You honestly didn't think a t-shirt could restrain me, did you?"

"Next time, I'll bring the cuffs." Her eyes flare at my words. She likes the idea. I file the information away for use later.

She grabs my cock and lifts herself up to align her center with it.

"Protection," I manage to grunt out.

"No need. I can't get pregnant, and we both know you got tested last month."

"How do you—"

My words are cut off when she slams herself down on me. My hands fly to her hips to try and slow her down. I'm going to blow in about two seconds if she continues to squeeze me this way.

"You were taking too long," she complains, but she stills to allow herself to adjust to my size.

I caress her hips. "All good things are worth waiting for."

She lifts herself up and pauses with the tip of me inside her. "I never did have much patience," she says before slamming herself down.

Two can play at this game. I lift my hips and thrust into her as she lowers. We quickly find a rhythm. Skin slaps against skin and our grunts and moans fill the room.

"Damn, Whiskey. You feel better than anything I've ever felt before."

In response, she squeezes my cock until I can't help but fall off the precipice I've been tottering on since the moment her warmth surrounded me.

"Lexi," I groan as sparks ignite throughout my body.

"Yes!" she cries as her movements become erratic. After a minute, she slows and then stops before collapsing on my chest. We lay there, gasping for breath, for several minutes.

"Phew," she says as she props her chin on her hand to gaze up at me. "You do know how to use that monster-sized thing after all."

I chuckle. "I love you." Her eyes widen. Her panic isn't far behind. I tuck a strand of hair behind her ear. "It's okay. You don't have to say it back."

"Say it back?" She scoffs. "I don't feel it back."

"Whatever you say, Lexi. Whatever you say."

I know how she feels. It's enough. For now.

Chapter 29

You think I'm crazy? You should see me with my best friend.

"Kɪss me before you go," Lenny demands.

I roll my eyes. "Stop ordering me around."

"You didn't seem to mind me ordering you around last night."

"Whatever," I mutter to hide the shiver his words cause.

He's done waiting as evidenced by him reaching across the front seat and wrapping his hand around my neck and dragging me near.

"Have a good day, Whiskey," he whispers against my mouth before briefly touching his lips to mine.

I pull away and open the door to the monster SUV before I decide to hell with work.

"Call me when you need a ride home."

"I'll hitch a ride." I slam the door before he can respond. I may have enjoyed him taking charge in the bedroom, but he's not in charge of me.

It's bad enough he insisted on driving me to work this morning. After I told him my plans to reveal my past to my friends, there wasn't a chance in hell he was letting me drive myself to work. Does he think I'm going to break down and need a ride home? He really doesn't know me well if he thinks breaking down is a possibility.

I whistle as I unlock the office and get ready for the day. When Hailey shows up fifteen minutes later, I smile and welcome her. "Happy Monday."

She pauses for a moment before stepping back and opening the door to announce down the corridor. "Hurry up, Phoebe! It's happened!"

But when the door opens next it's not Phoebe and her protector Ryker, it's an unknown man. I want to thank the man for delaying the interrogation Hailey is dying to begin but judging by the crazy in his eyes, this delay isn't going to be much fun.

"Welcome to *You Cheat, We Eat.* How can I help you?"

"Is this the PI firm?"

I indicate the seat in front of me. "It sure is."

He collapses in the chair. "Thank goodness. I need help with my girlfriend."

Hailey sighs before escaping to her office. Coward. Phoebe walks in and steps toward the man with her hand extended, but Ryker grabs hold of her and hauls her off to his office before slamming the door.

"Where were we, Mr. …?"

"Freddy. You can call me Freddy."

I remove an intake form from my top drawer. "How can we help you, Freddy?"

"My girlfriend's cheating on me."

I cringe. "I'm sorry."

"I need you to prove it."

"You want us to prove your girlfriend is cheating on you?" What the hell for? Dump her ass and be on your way is what I want to say, but I don't. Cheating partners is the bread and butter of the business after all.

He nods. "Yes."

"Okay." I tap my pen against the intake form. "We're going to need some information about your girlfriend."

"Oh, I'm positive you know everything about her already."

My hand freezes poised above the form. "I do?"

Does he think we're mind readers? Granted the government has been working on developing mind reading – a fact Suzie would kill to know, although I won't be telling her – but I have a feeling he doesn't think I can read his mind.

"Of course. Everyone knows Rihanna."

I study him. Despite the crazy words coming out of his mouth, except for the crazy eyes and talk, he doesn't appear crazy. His appearance says average thirty-something business-man, not man whose grip on reality has come undone. He's wearing a suit and tie, he's cleanshaven, and his hair is combed and styled. He appears to be on the way to his office, not the insane asylum.

"And Rihanna is your girlfriend?"

His smile spreads from ear to ear. "Yes, she is."

"Okay," I draw the word out while I try to think of an acceptable response to Mr. Lost The Plot's words. "And she's been cheating on you?"

He crosses his arms over his chest and frowns. "Yes, she's been photographed with some rapper."

I'll take him at his word since I don't follow celebrity gossip.

"And what do you want us to do?"

He throws his arms in the air. "Isn't it obvious? I want you to prove she's cheating."

Now, I'm curious. I can't help myself from asking, "And this will help you how?"

"She thinks I don't know about *him*." He practically spits out the word him. "Once she knows I know, she'll give him up and return to me."

Time to wrap this up. I stand. "I'm sorry, Freddy, but I'm afraid we can't help you."

He stands as well. "Why not?"

"Our PIs only work locally."

He frowns. "Oh. I guess I understand."

I open the door to him. "I hope you find someone to help you," I tell him as he leaves. I don't tell him I think it should be a psychiatrist.

"Why is it always Rihanna?" Hailey asks as she steps into the reception area.

I shrug. "Who do you expect it to be? Dolly Parton?"

Chrissie snorts as she joins us. "Please, you know you love Dolly."

Of course, I love Dolly. She's awesome. I don't say those words, though. Instead, I raise my voice and shout to Phoebe's husband. "You may want to leave the building, Ryker. I believe the girl talk is about to begin."

Phoebe rushes into the room. "I'm here!"

Ryker growls as he follows her. "No running."

She pats his chest. "I'm fine." Her stomach rumbles. "Actually, I'm hungry. Can you get me some pancakes?"

He kisses her forehead before leaving without saying another word.

"You're good," Hailey tells her.

Phoebe shrugs as she sits down. "I understand he's feeling super-protective with me being pregnant – especially since he's never had a family before – but there's a limit to how far I'll let him go. Being wrapped in shrink wrap is not a good look on anyone."

"Good for you," I tell her before turning to Chrissie. "Do you have some work for me?"

She laughs. "You know I'm here because Hailey sent me a message about 'the deed being done'."

My shoulders slump. Of course, Hailey did.

Chrissie rubs her hands together. "This is the first bet I've won. I can't wait to figure out what to do with my winnings."

"It's not Memorial Day yet," Phoebe complains.

"It's May. You had March. I'm way closer than you," Chrissie points out.

"I'm glad my love life amuses you."

Chrissie shrugs. "What can I say? I'm easily amused."

No, she's not. What she is, is a good friend who wants to make sure I'm ready before I reveal my past. I don't question how she knows I'm about to do a big revelation. I stopped wondering how she knows what's going to happen years ago.

She's a woman of many talents. Apparently, mindreading really is a thing.

I clear my throat. "I need to tell you something."

When the women recognize how serious my voice is, they settle down in chairs across from me. With their attention focused one-hundred percent on me, I'm not sure I can do this. Crap. I'll start with the good news and work my way back to Megan.

"William signed the divorce papers."

Chrissie jumps to her feet and rushes me. She crushes me in her arms and pretty soon Hailey and Phoebe join in to make it a group hug. I bask in the warmth of their friendship and use it to gather my courage.

"There's more," I tell them. I sit down – no way can I tell this story while standing – and begin. By the time I finish, Phoebe's sobbing.

She crushes me to her. "I'm sorry about Megan."

Hailey's reaction is the polar opposite. She seethes as she stomps around the room. "Is the piece of shit still in town? I say we go over there and give William a piece of our minds. And by piece of mind, I mean beat the daylights out of him. A bunch of girls beating him up will hurt his precious pride."

"He already left town," Chrissie announces. Of course, she's been keeping tabs on him. I should have known.

"I didn't tell you this to make everyone mad or sad."

Phoebe hiccups. "I'm pregnant. I'm allowed to be sad."

"Of course, you are," Hailey says and pats her shoulder while mouthing to us *Rollercoaster hormones.*

You'd think after telling them about Megan, this next part would be a piece of cake. It's not. I feel my face heat as I admit, "Lenny thinks I should see a counselor, and I may agree with him."

Chrissie whips out her phone. "I have the perfect woman for you to see. There's also a support group nearby. They meet at lunchtime on Thursdays. I've sent you the information."

My phone beeps in confirmation. I should have known Chrissie already did the necessary research. She always was two steps ahead of me when we worked together at the agency.

Hailey slaps Chrissie's arm. "Don't pressure her."

Chrissie snorts. "As if sending her information is pressuring her."

It kind of is, but it's the type of pressure I need. I hate to admit it, but Lenny's right. It's time to talk to someone about Megan's death. It will always be my fault she's no longer with us, but I need to find a way to live with my guilt.

It's not fair to the man who I love. No, not the man I love. The man who loves me. Shit. Do I love Lenny? I slap my forehead and force those thoughts out of my brain. I refuse to think about this right now. One hurdle at a time.

Chapter 30

There is nothing better than a friend. Unless it's a friend with a plan.

AT five minutes to five o'clock, Lenny struts into *You Cheat, We Eat* like he owns the place. I'm not complaining. The man can strut like no one's business. His age of fifty-seven is of no consequence. The man can strut.

He prowls right up to me, tags my hand, and yanks me out of my chair before laying a quick, close-mouthed kiss on me.

"What are you doing? I'm at work. Hailey or Phoebe could have seen." My admonishment doesn't sound very harsh considering I'm gasping for breath.

He smirks. "Hailey and Phoebe aren't here." How does he know? He didn't exactly scan the area before hauling me from my chair. "Besides, I spent the day getting razzed on by my brothers. There's no one left in our friend group who doesn't know what happened last night."

I shove him away. "Did you tell everyone we had sex last night?"

The humor in his eyes dies. "Whiskey, are you ashamed of me?"

I roll my eyes. "Of course not. But I don't kiss and tell."

He palms my neck. "Neither do I, sweetheart. Neither do I." His eyes laser in on my lips. As much as I know I'll enjoy where this is leading, this is my place of work.

I slam my hand against his mouth. "No hanky-panky at work."

He clears his throat. "Okay."

What? He's not going to fight me? He's going to listen to me and respect my choices? No wonder I love this man. Ugh. There's the L-word again. I push those thoughts out of my mind the same as I've done a hundred times today already. It's way too early for L-word declarations no matter what Lenny says.

"I-I-I…" I clear my throat. Way to sound smooth Lexi. "I need to shut down my computer and then I can leave."

"Anything I can do to help?"

"You can clean out the coffee grinds from the coffee machine and ready it for tomorrow morning," I suggest and ignore the warmth in my tummy at the idea of a man offering to help out instead of yelling at me to get my ass moving. Lenny is not William and it's unfair to continue to compare the two.

Five minutes later, we're driving out of the parking garage in Lenny's SUV. But when he exits the garage, he turns in the wrong direction.

"Where are we going? This isn't the way to my place. Are we going to your place?" I rub my hands together in anticipation. "I've never been to your place. What's it like? Do you live in a bat cave?"

He grunts. "Why would I live in a bat cave?"

I shrug and glance away. "Why else haven't I seen your place?"

He pulls over and stops on the side of the road. He grasps my chin and forces me to look his way. "I haven't been hiding where I live from you on purpose."

I raise an eyebrow. "But you have been hiding where you live on accident?"

"I—" He swears under his breath. "I didn't think of how this would feel for you. I'm an idiot."

I nod because when a man says he's an idiot, you always agree with him.

"I thought you'd be more comfortable in your place."

"Breaking this down what you really mean is you thought it'd be easier to seduce me in a place I'm comfortable in rather than in a place I don't know."

He blows out a breath of air. "I had to fall for a smart woman."

Flattery will get him nowhere. I don't let him off the hook. Not yet. "Well, what are you going to do to rectify this situation?"

"I guess we're sleeping at my place tonight," he announces and drops his hand before pulling out into traffic again.

"Who said *we're* sleeping anywhere together tonight?" I try to sound all indignant but it's difficult considering my skin is tingling in anticipation.

He rests his hand on my thigh and squeezes. "We'll see. We'll see."

"If we're not going to your place and we're not going to mine, where exactly are we going?"

"It's a surprise."

We drive out of the city and travel west. I don't know Wisconsin very well – I haven't taken the time to explore the surroundings much – so I have no idea where we could be going and what for. Which is fine with me. I trust Lenny. Whoa. I trust Lenny? Talk about scary.

"You're not taking me somewhere to give me a lobotomy so you can eat my brains, are you?" I ask to stop my mind from freaking out about trusting this man.

Lenny frowns. "That scene was too far-fetched for me."

"Huh. I'm not sure if we can be friends if you aren't a *Silence of the Lambs* fan."

"Oh, I'm a *Silence of the Lambs* fan, but there's a reason the sequel *Hannibal* was critically panned."

The man knows his movie references. Another check in the positive column. Those stupid checks are racking up.

He glances over at me. "And, Whiskey, we're way more than friends."

Since I'm not responding to his comment, we fall into silence for the rest of the drive. After an hour, Lenny pulls off the highway and drives through a small town before parking in a lot next to a lake. I jump out and scan the area.

"I don't know, boss. Nature area with no one around? This could definitely be a scene from some horror movie."

He throws a backpack at me. "You can change in the building over there." He points to a small wooden structure.

I unzip the bag to discover leggings, a long-sleeved t-shirt, and a sports bra. These are my clothes. My clothes that were in my drawers this morning. "You went through my clothes?"

"I could hardly surprise you if you packed yourself, now could I?"

"Whatever," I mumble and march off to the building to change. When I return, Lenny has some rope over his shoulder and is holding two harnesses and some carabiners.

"How do you know I can rock climb?"

He chuckles. "Knowing exactly what this equipment is for kind of gave you away." No, it didn't. I cross my arms over my chest and stare him down. "Fine. I asked Chrissie. You'll have to tell me about the time the two of you decided to race each other down the mountain."

Never going to happen. I love Chrissie to death, but the woman switches on my competitive drive like no one else can. And no one should be out rock climbing while drinking moonshine. Talk about stupid.

"Is it a set path or are we blazing our own trail?"

"No way are we free climbing until I know your skill level."

I lift an eyebrow. "Maybe it's me who needs to assess your skill level."

I'm totally trash talking. I've done some rock climbing, but I'm not an expert. I'm relieved we'll be doing an aided climb.

"Get suited up. We're losing light." He hands me a pair of rock climbing shoes and a helmet.

Once I'm ready, we hike a few hundred yards to an outcrop of rocks. We walk around the outcrop until we come to the opposite side with its cliff wall. The sixty-foot tall limestone rock is ideal for climbing. I step closer and note the rock has permanently-fixed bolts and anchors drilled into it. Awesome.

"You go first," Lenny says and hands me a harness.

"You just want to watch my ass while I climb and you belay," I quip.

His eyes flare and he steps closer. "Damn straight I do."

Yikes. I started something we can't finish right now. My entire body warms, but I resist the urge to fan myself. No sense letting Lenny know the effect he has on me. Judging by the smirk on his face, he already knows.

An hour later, I swallow a moan as I climb into the SUV. My arms and legs are burning from the exertion I put them through. Fun fact. Rock climbing uses your leg muscles as much as your arm muscles. Great. My whole body is going to be sore tomorrow.

Lenny whistles as he joins me in the vehicle. My eyes narrow at how comfortable he appears. Do his muscles not ache? What a jerk. He could at least pretend to be sore.

"You want to grab a bite to eat on the way home or do takeout?"

My stomach grumbles. I guess my hot bath is going to have to wait. "Let's hit up the drive-through."

I'm chowing down on a cheeseburger when Lenny clears his throat before asking, "How did the girls react to you telling them about Megan?"

I narrow my eyes on him. "How do you know I didn't chicken out?"

I'm no chicken, but what I am is not entirely comfortable with this topic of conversation.

He frowns. "Maybe because I spent the day fielding calls from their husbands asking me when we were driving down to West Virginia to handle William."

My nose scrunches. "Why would Aiden and Ryker want to handle William?"

"Don't you get it by now? Those men are as much your friends as their wives. Face it, Whiskey. You've been adopted into this makeshift, crazy family, and we're not letting you go."

Family? I gulp. I gave up on family a long time ago. When your parents force you to stay married to a man you hate with every breath of your body, you stop thinking of them as 'family'.

Chapter 31

True friendship is walking into a person's house and your Wi-Fi connecting automatically.

LENNY

"This is your place?" Lexi cranes her neck to peer out of the windshield at my house. "It's a mansion."

"It's not a mansion," I grumble. I'll admit the sprawling two-story ranch is big, but it's no mansion.

"It's not?" She motions to the house. "How many people live in there?"

A pain hits my chest, but I ignore it. I've had enough practice after all. "Just me."

Her eyes soften, and she reaches across the console to grasp my hand. "I'm sorry. I was being insensitive."

I sigh before admitting the truth to her. There's no sense trying to hide. She saw right through me to the pain I try to keep buried.

"I bought this place when I first arrived in Milwaukee after retiring from the Army. I thought I'd find a nice woman and fill it up with children." She squeezes my hand. "It never happened."

"I'm sorry. I know the feeling."

Normally, someone sympathizing with me would cause me to lash out, but not Lexi. What she suffered is twenty times worse than my pathetic love life. *Former* pathetic love life, I remind myself. Lexi is mine now, and I'm not letting her go.

I open my door. "Come on. Let me show you my home."

I round the vehicle to open the door for her. She lets me help her out for a change. I know it's because she's sore as hell, but I don't remark upon it. I'm not a stupid man.

"This house is…" She pauses. "It's gorgeous."

I put myself in her shoes and study the place as if it's my first time seeing it. The house is gray with white trim, but the front door is bright red. The front has a wraparound porch with a porch swing and two Adirondack chairs on it. To the right is an attached three-car garage, which I didn't use today as I wanted to open the front door for Lexi instead of letting her in via the garage; the way I usually enter the house.

I place my hand on Lexi's back and lead her toward the front door. I unlock the door and allow her to enter first.

She gasps before whirling around on me. "How did you…?"

I guide her further into the house and close the door behind us. There are candles lit on every available surface in the living room. A fire is blazing in the fireplace and a dozen red roses are set in a crystal vase on the coffee table.

There's also a bottle of champagne chilling in a bucket with a plate of chocolate-covered strawberries next to it. Someone went beyond her brief considering I didn't order either one of those.

"Who are you and what have you done with my Lenny?"

Her Lenny? I'll pay Chrissie to romanticize my house every day of the week as long as Lexi continues to claim me as hers.

"And how did you manage this?" I don't bother to respond. "You called Chrissie when I went to the restroom at the fast food place, didn't you?"

I nod. There's no sense denying it.

Her eyes narrow. "Does Chrissie have a key to your house? Why has she seen your house and I haven't?"

Damn. I didn't realize this would upset her. I wrap an arm around her waist and pull her near until she's cradled to my chest. Too bad we're both fully clothed.

"Chrissie doesn't have a key to my house. Wally does, although we both know he doesn't need a key to gain entry." I wait for her nod before continuing. "And Chrissie hasn't been to my house before today."

I kiss her nose, which is scrunched up again. "And I'm truly sorry I haven't invited you over before today. It was merely an oversight, I promise."

"I guess I can forgive you. Seeing as you went to all this trouble. Oh wait, you didn't do this. You asked someone to." She taps her chin. "Hm…"

"I paid for it."

"I guess we shouldn't let it go to waste then." She wiggles to escape my hold. "I can't wait to see you drink champagne from those dainty flutes."

I tighten my hold on her and shake my head. "You're having a bath first."

She waggles her eyebrows. "Want to get me naked, do you, Mr. Walker?"

My cock twitches. Hell yeah, he says. I'm on board with this plan. I tell him to calm down. Lexi's sore from climbing. She'll never admit it, but she is. And I want her sore for an entirely different reason. But first I need to treat her aches and pains from climbing.

"I want you all relaxed and warm," I say.

"You can get me hot and bothered instead."

I step back and smack her ass. "Bath first. Shenanigans latter."

"Shenanigans? No one says shenanigans anymore, old man."

"Old man? Who you calling an old man?"

I don't wait for her to reply before throwing her over my shoulder and prowling to the stairs. She struggles in my hold until I spank her ass. Then, she squirms for an entirely different reason. I file the information away for use later.

Lexi's head lifts as we walk past the doors in the hallway to the furthest room.

"How many bedrooms does your mansion have anyway?"

I know she's teasing, but I answer. "Five. I use one as a gym and one as my office."

"Office. I hope I don't get called into the principal's office for being a bad girl."

Lexi enjoys playing, does she? I am on board. But first, a bath.

I open the door to my bedroom. Lexi gasps. "Holy cow. This room is huge."

She's not wrong. There's a California king bed against one wall. Despite the size of the bed, there's plenty of additional space. In front of the bay window, I added a reading space with two armchairs and a shared ottoman.

"Is this where you have your orgies?"

Shit. I set her down on her feet and maneuver her until she's backed up against the wall and has no choice but to look at me. I pinch her chin.

"No one but me has ever slept on this bed."

She rolls her eyes. "Do you seriously expect me to believe you?"

"It's true. I bought a new mattress after I met you."

Her nose scrunches and her eyes narrow. "Awful sure of yourself, aren't you?"

I wasn't, but I also wasn't going to chance having her here and making her sleep on a bed she wouldn't be comfortable in.

"I also bought new sheets and a new comforter."

Her eyes widen. "I don't want to know what you did to make you feel you needed to buy a new comforter."

"Smart ass. I didn't do anything with the comforter. I wanted a clean slate."

"You still kept the humongous bed, though."

I step closer until I can feel her breasts straining against my chest. "Whiskey, I need room to maneuver."

Her eyes dilate until the whiskey color is practically invisible, and her chest heaves against mine. Oh yeah, she more than likes the idea of play. Perfect. The woman is perfect for me. I'm tempted to throw her on the bed right now and have my wicked way with her, but first, she needs her bath. I nab her hand and lead her to the attached bathroom.

Her jaw falls open when she enters. I don't know if it's the size of the bathroom or the bathtub filled to the rim with bubble bath and rose petals. There are more candles in here as well.

"Do you like the bathroom?"

If she doesn't, I'll have the contractor here to gut it next week. This will be Lexi's home as soon as I can convince her to move in, and I want her to love it as much as I do.

She skims her hand along the marble vanity. "Are you kidding? Double sinks. Marble everywhere. A shower large enough for the entire starting line-up of the Green Bay Packers and a tub big enough for the rest of the team. Of course, I love it."

I fit my front to her back and direct her attention to the bathtub. "What about this? Do you like this?"

"You didn't have to do all this, you know. I'm not a girl who needs romance."

I whirl her around and caress her cheek. "Whiskey, you may not need romance, but you sure as hell deserve it."

Her eyes sparkle at my words and her cheeks heat.

"I want to give the woman I love everything she deserves."

She rolls her eyes. "You're pouring it on awful thick, old man."

I roll my hips into her stomach to allow her to feel my hardness. Her breath hitches.

"Who are you calling an old man?"

"Being able to swallow a blue pill doesn't make you younger," she quips.

"No blue pill necessary, my love. All I need is you. I love you."

Her mouth drops open. "I, um, I …"

I place a finger over her mouth. "Shush. I know you're not ready yet. It's okay. I can be a patient man."

She snorts. "Patient, my ass."

I slap that very ass. "Go enjoy your bath before I forget about being a gentleman and have my wicked way with you."

She bites her bottom lip. "Wicked way?"

I use my teeth to free her lip. "I promise to do all sorts of wicked things to you," I whisper against her lips before stepping back. "As soon as you've had your bath."

She whips her t-shirt off to reveal her pink sports bra. The bra pushes her breasts up and my fingers tingle to touch her. She unsnaps her jeans and I whirl around.

"Chicken."

I'm not a chicken, but my restraint is vanishing quicker than she can reveal her creamy skin.

"I'm getting your champagne." And then I'm going to join her in the tub. A man can only restrain himself so far.

Chapter 32

True friends don't say they have your back. They just do.

"WHAT IS MOBY DICK's dad's name?" Barney waggles his eyebrows as he looks around our table at McGraw's Pub.

"Papa Boner," Val answers.

The couple high-five each other as if they planned the whole scenario. Knowing them, they probably did. Val is crazy, and Barney isn't far behind her on the crazy scale.

I lean forward. "Why does it take one-hundred million sperm to fertilize one egg?"

Barney rubs his hands together in anticipation. I make him wait.

"Because they won't stop to ask directions."

Chrissie and Val giggle at my joke while Wally and Barney scowl.

"Since when do you know dirty jokes?" Lenny asks.

"Um, hello. There's this thing called Google. I'll show it to you sometime, old man."

He growls like he does every single time I call him old man. His growl causes my insides to heat up in anticipation, which is the whole reason why I continue to call him an old man in the first place. I never knew having a partner could be this much fun.

The door to the pub flies open and someone screeches, "Where is she?"

I bury my face in my hands. I know that voice. It's the last voice on the earth I want to hear when I'm out with my boyfriend on a Saturday night having a good time. The voice is the ringing of the death knell on good times.

Lenny rubs my neck. "Who is it?"

"Momma and Papa dearest," I mumble from behind my hands.

I blow out a puff of air before dropping my hands and straightening my back. I better deal with them before they shout the place down. I shove at Lenny to let me out of the booth. He moves to allow me to stand, but he doesn't go far. He captures my hand, and we march together toward the door.

"If I were you, I'd run for the hills," I mutter to him.

"Never surrender."

"It's your funeral."

I stop in front of my parents. I haven't seen them in a few years – ever since my lovely momma insisted I was a stepmother to William and Ellie's children – and they are looking worse for wear. It makes sense. They aren't the youngest anymore. Even having had me as teenagers, they're still getting up there in age.

"Hello," I greet them with no enthusiasm in my voice whatsoever.

"Hello? Don't you hello me, young lady."

I wrinkle my brow and feign confusion at my mother's reaction. "What should I say?"

"I vote for leave and never return," Lenny says, and my father turns his scowl on him.

"Who is this man? Are ya stepping out on William?"

I throw my arms in the air. "Are you serious? William is living with another woman. You should know. You invited her to Christmas dinner last time I visited."

Lenny growls, and I pat his chest to calm him down. Judging by the scowl on his face, it didn't work.

"If ya'd come home, William would stop messing around with Ellie."

I cross my arms over my chest. "One, I am home. Two, William was messing around with Ellie when I lived with him. I highly doubt he's going to quit messing around with her anytime soon."

My mother's lips purse as she surveys the place. "Ya can't possibly call this place home."

"Obviously, I don't live in a pub, but Milwaukee is my home."

Huh. Would you look at that? I'm not lying. Milwaukee was supposed to be a pit stop while I figured out my life, but somewhere along the way, it became home. I peek over at Lenny. I'd blame him, but the friends I can feel at my back have a lot to do with my finding my forever home as well.

"Y'all can't possibly wanna live here in the city." She doesn't try to disguise her disgust.

"I've been living in the city for more than two decades, because – spoiler alert – I enjoy living in the city."

Don't get me wrong. I do miss the beauty of the nature in the holler – it's unlike anything you'll see anywhere else in the world – but live there? Not on your life.

"Y'all need to make up with William."

"Am I hallucinating?" I ask Lenny. "Do you put acid in my beer or something? Because there's no possible way my momma told me I need to make up with the man who nearly caused me to die."

A chorus of growls begins behind me. I hold up my hand to stop them. This is my fight. I'm happy to have them at my back supporting me, but this is my fight. Yes, I'm repeating myself, but it bears repeating.

Lenny tucks a strand of hair behind my ear. "No, love. You're not hallucinating."

"Damn. I guess my parents are as delusional as they've always been then."

My father clears his throat. "We're right here. We can hear everything you're saying."

"You can?" I widen my eyes and feign surprise. "It sure doesn't seem as if you can hear me. You haven't heard me for all these years as I've explained again and again how I will never be with a man who hurt me the way he did."

Momma sighs. "Y'all need to stop beating a dead horse. Ya didn't die. Y'all standing right here in front of me."

I lunge forward, but Lenny captures me before I can wring her neck. "I didn't die, but Megan did."

"Megan? Who's Megan?"

"Lady, you better wise the hell up before I let your daughter loose," Lenny orders.

"You need to get your hands off my daughter," my father orders. "She's a married woman."

"No!" I shout. "I am not! William signed the divorce papers. As soon as the court approves them, we will be divorced. Don't tell me y'all don't know this. It's the entire reason y'all drove your sorry asses up here. Y'all don't leave the holler for nothing."

I struggle against Lenny's hold, but he keeps his arms banded around me with all his strength. I can get out of his hold, but not without hurting him and the last thing I want to do is hurt the man I love. Crap on a cracker. Now is not the moment to have a revelation about my feelings for Lenny. I shove those thoughts in the back of my mind for consideration later.

"I vote we let Lexi free to whoop their asses," Wally says from behind me. "Who's with me?"

"I will put you over my knee and tan your ass if you disrespect me again. I am your daddy, and you will respect me."

Pain slashes through me at his words. Daddy? He's never been a parent to me. Granted he was practically a child when I was born but still. He could have at least tried to be a dad, but he never did. No more than Momma tried to be a mother.

My shoulders sag, and I give up the fight. What's the point? They never hear what I have to say anyway.

"You can let me go. I'm done."

Lenny loosens his hold on me to wrap an arm around my shoulders and pull me near.

"I will never let you go, love." He kisses my hair.

"You know, William has money. This man…" My father's lip curls as he scans Lenny up and down. "… don't look like he can keep a roof above your head."

Lenny barks out a laugh. "Wrong," he tells them once his laughter subsides. "I'm comfortable."

"Do ya have any idea how much William is worth?" My father doesn't know when to quit. He also doesn't bother to mention how William's money is anything but clean.

"Don't know. Don't care. You're welcome to review my portfolio, though."

"Are you crazy?" I ask him. "Why would you offer them that opportunity?"

He rubs his nose against mine. "They're never going to accept my offer."

Oh yeah. True.

"Momma, Papa, you should go now." The words momma and papa feel wrong in my mouth, but I'm not going to incite their anger further by calling them by their first names. My priority right now is getting them to leave.

Suzie pushes her way to the front of the crowd. Grayson sighs but follows behind her. She stops directly in front of my parents.

"You give parents a bad name." She rubs her belly. "My girl—"

"Boy," Grayson corrects, and Suzie glances over her shoulder to stick her tongue out at him.

"My child will never know how it feels to be unloved the way you're making Lexi feel right now." She grabs my hand and squeezes. "Lexi girl, you are loved. These people are nothing."

"Um, thank you?"

Who is this woman? Suzie is the klutzy, crazy woman; not the sweet woman who makes my eyes itch.

My parents survey the group as if they only now realize we're surrounded. "Who are these people?" Momma spits out the question.

"This my real family." I step forward to glare down at my parents. "A real family who has my back whenever I need it. A real family who laugh and joke together."

"And give each other shit," Suzie adds. There's my crazy girl.

"And tell each other dirty jokes," Val chimes in.

"And drink tequila shots together," Hailey says.

"And try wedding cake together," Faith says.

"And set up romantic surprises for each other," Chrissie says.

Enough! "Are all y'all trying to embarrass me?"

"No, but it was worth it to hear your West Virginian drawl come out to play. It's sexy," Lenny whispers in my ear.

I roll my eyes. "What don't you find sexy?"

"If it's you, it's sexy. Every single thing about you is sexy."

"But the arrangement," my father interrupts.

Wrong thing to say. The good mood of the crowd evaporates immediately.

Suzie glances over her shoulder at me. "He did not seriously mention the agreement where they profit and you suffer for your entire life, did he? Because I can take him. No one hits a pregnant woman."

Grayson grabs her and hauls her away. "Enough for you, Munchkin."

"It's Mighty Munchkin!" she argues.

"I'm done, Whiskey. Get them to leave or I will."

I lift up on my tiptoes to kiss Lenny's lips. "They're all yours."

I'm not lying. I do an about-face and walk back to the table with the women following me. The men stay at the door to deal with my sperm and egg donor as Momma and Papa shall henceforth be known.

"Are you okay?" Chrissie asks.

I force a smile. "I am."

I'm not exactly lying. Am I embarrassed Momma and Papa just put on a shitshow of a showdown at the bar I frequent? Yep. But I'm also feeling all warm and fuzzy with how my friends had my back. Friends? These people are more than friends. They're my family.

Chapter 33

What's the meaning of a true friend? Someone who brings homemade pepperoni rolls to your barbeque.

I allow Lenny to help me out of his SUV since I'm holding a tray of my homemade pepperoni rolls. Fine. If I'm being completely truthful, I let him pretend to be a gentleman more often. Since my parents showed up and he ran them out of town, I've given up on my stubbornness – not completely, because it is awfully fun sometimes, but I have let Lenny in more and more.

I do love the man after all, although I haven't told him my feelings yet – see comment about being stubborn above – but I'm pretty sure he knows how I feel.

"Shall I take the plate for you?" he says and reaches out for it.

I slap his hand away. "Stop trying to steal a pepperoni roll."

"But they smelled delicious while you were baking them," he pouts.

I wink. "Because they are."

"Now, you're just being mean."

I giggle as he opens the gate for Val and Barney's backyard where we're having a Memorial Day barbeque. We don't make it two steps into the yard before Val cries, "Someone check her ring finger!"

"I got it!" Chrissie smiles as she saunters up to us.

I wave my left hand – including my bare ring finger – at her. "Someone's a loser."

She snorts. "Not hardly. I have July 4th."

Lenny kisses my cheek and nabs the plate out of my hand. "Let me set these down on the table for you."

"Thief!" I shout after him. He ignores me as he's too busy stealing a roll from the plate. Typical man.

Chrissie threads her arm through mine and draws me further into the yard. "How are you doing?" I give her a blank look. "You know, since mommy and daddy dearest visited."

It's been a few weeks since the whole showdown at McGraw's Pub. Lenny has kept his eye on me the whole time. He tries to be subtle, but I'm not an idiot. I see him watching me, waiting for me to fall apart. I'm not about to fall apart. I'm free.

"I'm fine."

She frowns; clearly not believing my words.

"I am," I insist. "The break with my family was a long time coming."

"But you seemed happy the time I spent Christmas with you in West Virginia."

"I have two words for you. Moonshine and twenty years."

It's been twenty years since Chrissie and I celebrated Christmas with my family in the holler. I won't deny I had a good time. But enjoying being 'back home' for a few days during the holidays is completely different than actually living there and confronting all the hurts your family has done to you.

To Chrissie's credit, she nods and agrees with me before leaning close to whisper, "You didn't happen to bring any moonshine with you, did you?"

I pull my flask out of my jacket pocket and wave it in her face. "What do you think?"

"No." Wally appears in front of me. Where did he come from? I tell you the man can move without making any sound. It's creepy. I'm super jealous.

Chrissie juts out her bottom lip and pouts. "But it's a holiday."

He crosses his arms over his chest and glares down at her. "The last time you drank moonshine, you tore your clothes off in my truck before proceeding to streak into the house while screaming *You can't catch me. I'm the gingerbread man.*"

"Sounds like fun to me."

Chrissie winks at me. "It totally was."

Lenny saunters over and throws his arm around my shoulders. I point to the corner of his mouth. "You have a little something right there."

He licks his lip. "Whiskey, why haven't you made those rolls for me before?"

"Did you not notice how I spent all morning making dough?" I complain, but the real reason I don't make the pepperoni rolls more often is my penchant to eat the entire batch in one sitting.

He leans close to whisper in my ear, "I'll make it worth your while."

I shiver. I know he will. But I'm not easy. "Will you still make it worth my while when I weigh three-hundred pounds from eating all the rolls?"

He waggles his eyebrows. "Don't worry. I know how we can work those calories off."

"Perv." I elbow him.

"Come sit down," Suzie yells over at us. "My belly's too big to move and my feet are swollen to the size of Ronald McDonald's shoes."

I kiss Lenny before joining Suzie. Chrissie follows.

"How are you feeling?" I ask.

"Like my skin is going to explode from the pressure at any moment."

"Can I get you a drink? A bite to eat?"

She pushes to her feet but then grunts and plops back down on her chair. "Can you help me to the bathroom?"

Chrissie grabs her right side and I grab her left. Together, we haul Suzie to her feet. I hear a whooshing sound and glance down at the ground to notice Suzie's feet are now wet.

"Um, Suzie, I think your water broke."

She sighs. "I guess I'm too late for the bathroom."

I survey the area, but I don't see Grayson near. Normally, the man doesn't let his wife out of his sight. Where is he? "Grayson!" I scream.

He runs out of the house to the patio. "What is it?"

"It's time to welcome your baby into the world. Suzie's water broke."

His eyes widen and the bottles of soda in his hands crash to the ground. "You're in labor! You couldn't tell me you were in labor?"

"I didn't know I was in labor until my water broke, you big doofus." She groans before bending over at the waist and panting.

I rub her back as Chrissie supports her weight. Grayson rushes over to us. He falls to his knees and squeezes her hands.

"Just breathe, Precious. Just breathe through it."

The panting stops, and she gives him a dazzling smile. "It's time to welcome our baby into the world."

Grayson gets to his feet and lifts her into his arms. Aiden jingles his keys in their direction. "I'll drive. Where's her bag?"

"I'm right here. I'm having a baby, not deaf."

Grayson ignores her to answer Aiden. "Her bag's in the trunk of our car."

Hailey rushes off to their car while Aiden leads Grayson to his with everyone following. Suzie waves like a queen from the backseat where she's cradled in her husband's arms as we watch them drive away.

"Okay!" Val claps her hands. "Let's pack up the food."

"Pack up the food?" Barney asks. "What are you talking about?"

"If you think I'm letting my friend have a baby and not be there, think again, Mister."

Barney raises his hands in surrender. "Whatever you want, Trouble."

I guess we're having a picnic in the hospital.

Within thirty minutes, we're sitting in the hospital waiting room with the food spread out on several tables, but no one's eating. Everyone's staring at the door anxious for news about the newest addition to our family.

A nurse saunters past but halts when she notices the picnic. "What do you think you're doing? This isn't a park."

Faith picks up a plate. "Can I offer you some potato salad? A brat? Or maybe a pepperoni roll?"

"Hey!" Lenny grunts. "The pepperoni rolls are for me."

I elbow him in the stomach. "I'll make you some more." His eyes glitter with victory. I walked right into his maneuverings.

"I could eat," the nurse says as Faith hands her the loaded plate with a plastic fork.

"There's plenty for everyone," Faith says.

"Any news on the Neill baby?" Hailey asks before the nurse can escape.

"Grayson Eliot Neill, if you don't stop hovering around me, I'll kick you out of this room," Suzie screams.

"Never mind," Hailey mutters.

Lenny rubs his hands together. "What are you excited about?" I ask him.

"Sid is already out of the running."

I sigh. They're betting again. I should have known. "What's the bet?"

"How quickly Suzie will start swearing."

"It's not fair. Mary Ann said all the women giving birth swear," Sid pouts.

Speaking of Mary Ann, she peeks her head in the room and smiles when she sees us gathered around. "Awesome. I'm starving." She makes a beeline for the food.

"Aren't you going to greet your husband?" Sid asks.

"Yeah. Yeah." She waves at him. "Let me get a bite to eat first. I've been on my feet for six hours now."

Sid hears six hours, and his tune immediately changes. He grabs the plate from her and motions for her to sit down. She collapses in a chair, and he piles food onto the plate for her. He hands her the food with a bottle of water before sitting next to her.

"Do you need me to rub your feet?"

Mary Ann shakes her head. "Thanks, but no thanks. If I remove my clogs at this point, I'll never get them back on."

Sid frowns. "You work too much."

She shrugs in response as she shovels food in her mouth.

"You can take your ice chip and shove it up your bum where the sun doesn't shine," Suzie shouts from somewhere down the hall.

Max groans. "I'm out."

Lenny chuckles. "I don't know why anyone bothers to bet against me. I always win."

His words are barely out before Suzie shouts again, "That's it! Out, you big oaf! And don't come back."

Grayson stumbles into the waiting room looking like he's been punched in the gut. "She kicked me out."

"Don't worry," Mary Ann says around a mouthful of food. "She'll be screaming for you to return in about two minutes."

She groans around a bite of the pepperoni roll. "Where did you buy these?"

I narrow my eyes on her. "Those aren't store bought. I made them."

"Where's my husband? Did he abandon me? Does he not love me now I'm fat? I'm having his baby!" Grayson's eyes bug out at how hysterical his wife sounds.

Wally claps him on the back. "Get back in there, soldier."

Grayson gulps before straightening his back and starting to march away. Before he can leave, I shove a bottle of water in his hand. He nods his thanks and rushes out.

"Welp." Mary Ann gets to her feet. "I need to get back to work." She waves as she leaves with Sid chasing after her.

Once they're gone, we settle into our chairs to wait for the baby.

"Am I hungry? Are you crazy? I'm squeezing a watermelon out of a tiny hole and you're talking about food? What's wrong with you?"

Lenny checks his watch and grins. "Pay up, suckers."

Wally, Max, and Barney slap five-dollar bills into his hand.

"You can stop gloating any second now," I tell him.

He smirks. "Not a chance."

"Motherhumper son of a donkey!"

"You're almost there. One more push." Grayson's shout is nearly as loud as Suzie's.

"One more push? I'll show you one more push."

Grayson's response is drowned out by the cry of a child. Tears well in my eyes, and I look over at Lenny to see him blink the wetness in his eyes away. He kisses my nose before whispering, "I love you, Alexis Mullins."

I kiss his lips to avoid telling him I love him. I might return his feelings, but I've never told a man I've loved him before and a hospital waiting room is hardly the place to tell a man you love him for the first time.

Everyone stands when Grayson enters the room fifteen minutes later with a pink bundle in his arms. "I'd like you to meet Elizabeth Armela Neill."

Hailey gasps at the name, but I'm clueless. I raise a brow at Lenny, and he mouths *tell you later.*

Phoebe groans as she stands, and everyone's gaze turns to her. She waves her hands in front of her. "I'm not having my baby now. I'm sore from sitting is all."

"I told you we should have gone home," Ryker grumbles.

I ignore their bickering to have a closer look at the baby. "She's beautiful."

"You want to hold her?"

I'm surprised Grayson would let me hold his brand-new baby, but I don't question him. There's a pang in my chest as I cradle the baby and thoughts of Megan try to intrude. I don't let them. Now is not the time to be melancholic over what could have been.

"You okay?" Lenny whispers in my ear.

"I'm good." He doesn't appear to believe me. "Promise."

He kisses my forehead before reaching forward to skim a finger along baby Elizabeth's cheek. "She's a beauty."

"She's perfect," I whisper as I rock her.

"I want to hold her," Hailey pushes her way to me, and I hand the baby off to her.

Chapter 34

Best friends know how crazy you are and still
choose to be seen with you in public.

"It's quiet without Suzie and Phoebe around," Hailey complains as she scans McGraw's Pub.

Quiet? Even without the two of them and their husbands around, our group consists of twelve people. It's not exactly small. Plus, there are other patrons scattered throughout the bar despite it being Sunday lunchtime. The crowd will pick up even more in an hour when the football pre-game starts.

"Who's up for a game of darts?" Chrissie asks as she walks up to us.

I stand. "I'm up for kicking your ass in darts."

She smirks. "You're welcome to try."

"What game do you want to play?" I ask when we enter the back room where the dartboards and pool tables are located. "Traditional 501, Cricket?"

"Let's make this interesting. Let's play Around the Clock."

I shrug as if it doesn't matter what game we play. And it doesn't. I've been playing darts in bars since I was tall enough to peek over the counter. There wasn't a whole lot of ID-checking back in the holler. And, unlike my pool game, I've kept up with darts.

"What are we playing for?"

"Your pepperoni roll recipe."

She'll never get the recipe. In the extremely unlikely event I lose, I'll find some recipe online and give it to her.

"What do I get if I win?"

"I'll help you when you move into Lenny's house."

"No deal. You'll help me move anyway."

"Ha!" She points at me. "You didn't deny you're moving in with Lenny."

What can I say? At some point, I assume we'll move in together. I glance over at the table where Lenny is hanging out with his brothers. He smirks at me. Damn. I guess he heard.

I roll my eyes and feign indifference. "Whatever. Are we going to do this or are we going to gossip like a pair of old hags?"

She bumps my hip. "The living together thing isn't bad. Maybe you should try it." She waggles her eyebrows at Wally who winks in response.

"Gossip like old hags it is. Have you seen little Lizzie?"

"What an adorable baby. Her namesake was there when I visited."

Suzie continues to surprise me. I didn't expect her to name her first daughter after the wife of Grayson's fallen comrade. The man he apparently blamed himself for the death of and was riddled with guilt over. I never thought of Suzie as the woman to cure a man of his guilt, but she did.

"I'll play the winner," Lenny announces as he and Wally join us.

I rub my hands together. "Prepare to lose, old man."

Around the Clock is a darts game where each player has to throw a dart in every segment of the board exactly like a clock. Chrissie hands me a set of darts and we each take a turn throwing with our non-dominant hands to determine who starts.

Of course, it's me. I throw three darts and quickly move through three numbers. I smirk as I motion for Chrissie to go. She misses the one on the first try and has to try again. I feel my lips tip up at her mistake.

Lenny wraps his arm around me. "Don't be smug. You can still lose."

I'll burn McGraw's Pub down before I let Chrissie win. Slight exaggeration, but I do hate to lose – especially to Chrissie.

We continue around the clock for the next thirty minutes. Chrissie is better at darts than I gave her credit for. She's catching up to me, but I throw a twenty-five and bullseye to win.

I throw my hands in the air. "Take that, loser. I am the champion!"

She slaps her darts in Lenny's hand. "Good luck winning against Ms. Cheater here."

"I'm not a cheater, but you're a loser," I tease.

She tosses her hair over her shoulder before marching over to sit on Wally's lap. I look around and notice all of our friends are now watching us. Except for Max. He's manning the bar as the crowd has picked up.

"What are we playing for?" I ask Lenny with a waggle of my eyebrows.

"If I win, I get to tie you up for fifteen minutes," he growls into my ear. My belly warms at the idea of him tying me up again. I'm not usually submissive in any area of my life, but when Lenny takes control in the bedroom? I'm up for whatever games he wants to play.

Val giggles and I glance over Lenny's shoulder to find her fanning her face. "They're playing for sexual favors." She drops her hand to slap Barney.

"What? What did I do?"

"You never play games with me to win sexual favors."

"Trouble, you can have all the sexual favors you want. There's no need to play games."

"Our friends all have sex on the brain," I whisper to Lenny.

He cocks an eyebrow. "Our friends?"

Okay. Maybe I have sex on the brain, too. But look at my man. He's the very definition of sexy. His age is of no consequence. I catch younger women and men giving him the once over all the time.

"Let's play."

The game is neck and neck the entire time. I'm starting to worry when we're level at the twenty. Only the twenty-five and bullseye remain, and it's Lenny's turn. Damn. He's got three tries. The first try hits the twenty-five, and I feel sweat break out on my brow. How did I not know he's this good at darts?

"I'm going to win," he says with a wink.

I'm pretty sure we'll both win if he ties me up to the bed, but I still hate to lose.

He throws his second dart and hits twenty-five again. I cross my fingers. One more miss and I'm back in business.

He throws again and it's another twenty-five. I scowl at him. "Are you letting me win?"

"You haven't won yet." He nods toward the board. "Grab the darts for me, will you?"

I frown but do his bidding. When I pull the third dart out, something falls, and I rush to catch it. What the hell? I look down at the object in my hand and my eyes widen. A ring? A diamond ring? How the hell did it get there?

I whirl around to ask Lenny what's going on only to discover him on his knee. My eyebrows fly off my forehead. "What's going on?"

"Alexis Mullins, will you marry me?"

My heart stops. I want to scream yes. Here, in front of all my friends turned family, I want to say I'll marry this man I love, but I can't.

"But we haven't had the talk." The talk I'm dreading with all of my being.

"What do you mean? What talk?"

I grasp his hand, pull him to his feet, and drag him through the room. As I pass the bar, Max throws a set of keys at me. "Use my office."

I don't speak until we're secluded behind the locked office door.

"What's going on? Why are you stalling? I love you, I know you love me, what's the problem?"

"I do love you." I pause. Lenny steps forward with a smile on his face. I raise a hand to stop him.

"But we need to discuss your bi-sexuality."

His head whips back. "You said you didn't have a problem with my sexual orientation."

I wave my hands at him. "Of course, I don't. You misunderstand me."

"Explain."

I sigh. "It's just …" I wring my hands. "Am I enough for you? Just me? Don't you need…" I clear my throat. "Um… men to completely satisfy you."

"This is what you're worried about? This is why you haven't told me you love me before?"

"No. No. No. It's just I've never told a man I love him." Even to me, the words sound lame. My shoulders slump. "Okay. Fine. Maybe I've held back because I'm worried I'm not enough for you."

"Whiskey, my love." He cups my chin. "You're all I want. You're all I see. I wouldn't have asked you to marry me if I wasn't certain."

I bite my lip. "You are one-hundred percent sure? You're not going to change your mind and need to find relief in another person's arms?"

"Fuck." He growls. "I'm going to West Virginia and I'm going to kill William Harper. And it'll be nice and slow."

"I'm with you," Sid shouts through the door.

I glare at it. "They seriously couldn't leave us alone for five minutes?"

It's Barney's turn to shout. "Have you not met us?"

"I got ya, girl," Val yells before I hear what sounds like a stampede rushing down the hallway.

"Love," Lenny murmurs, and I return my attention to him. "I'm sorry. I didn't realize how William's betrayal still plays on your mind. I should have been more mindful."

"I'm over him." He raises an eyebrow. "I am. I promise. But I'm in unchartered territory here. I have no problem with you enjoying both women *and* men in the bedroom, but I do have a problem with the idea of you needing a man when you're with me."

He caresses my cheek. "I promise, Whiskey. The only person I need is standing right in front of me."

"You promise?" He nods. "On penalty of me cutting off your balls if you're lying?" He winces but manages to nod again.

I inhale and let my breath out slowly. "Okay, then. Ask me again."

"Will you marry me, Lexi?"

"No," I scowl. "The proper way."

He chuckles as he drops to one knee. He grasps my left hand in both of his. "Alexi Mullins, I love your stubborn ass. Will you marry me and spend the rest of your life with me making me pepperoni rolls?"

"Yes to the marriage, but you can learn how to make your own dang pepperoni rolls."

He slides the ring onto my finger and kisses my hand before springing to his feet. He picks me up and spins me around.

"But this means you forfeit in darts, and I win."

"Love, you already won." His lips briefly touch my forehead before he shouts, "She said yes!"

My cheeks heat. "They're still listening at the door?"

"Ignore them."

"I guess you're going to have to help me move earlier than you expected, Chrissie," I shout through the door.

Lenny laughs before his head dips and his lips meet mine, and all thoughts of our friends and their never-ending nosiness fly right out of my head.

Chapter 35

Nothing beats friendship. Except a friendiceberg.

LENNY

I carry the last of Lexi's boxes into my house and set it down in the living room. I expected the place to be full of boxes, but it's not.

"Are you sure this is everything?"

She rolls her eyes. "For the millionth time, I'm sure." Her nose scrunches. "Does it bother you I don't have much stuff?"

I shrug, although it does bother me. Lexi should have everything she wants. Three suitcases of clothes and a couple boxes of miscellaneous things is not enough.

She opens her arms wide to indicate the house. "Because I think you have enough for the two of us."

I wrap my arms around her waist and lift her to twirl her around. "I'm glad you're all moved in Mrs. Soon to be Walker."

She taps on my shoulder for me to let her down. "What do you mean Mrs. Walker? Are you assuming I'm taking your name? You know what they say about assumptions…"

I knew my stubborn girl would fight me on this. Time to have the talk. "I want you to have my last name," I tell her. Her lips purse, but I speak before she has the chance to start complaining. "Let me explain." She sighs and motions for me to continue.

"I don't want you to carry the name of your sperm donor any longer. I don't want you to think of him or your egg donor each and every time you say your name or scrawl your signature. I don't want you to be reminded of them ever again."

She blows out a puff of air. "How is it you turned a total macho alpha move into a sweet gesture?"

I grin. "Because I'm a sweet guy."

"What you mean is—" She stops when her phone beeps. As she reads the message, a huge smile breaks out over her face. "Guess what?" She doesn't give me a chance to guess. "Phoebe's having her baby." She squeals. "We're getting another baby in the family!"

"I guess this means we're going to the hospital."

"Of course, it does, Grumpy Bear."

Damn straight, I'm grumpy. I was planning on christening every room in the house, starting with the living room in five minutes. I put a pin in those plans. "Get your purse. I'll lock up."

Thirty minutes later, we find ourselves in the same waiting room as a few weeks ago except now Suzie and little Lizzie are sitting with us while Phoebe has her baby and Ryker loses his mind.

"I hope you didn't bet on Phoebe swearing while in labor," Lexi mumbles to me.

"Nope."

Her eyes narrow. "But you bet on something. What is it?"

"How long it takes for Ryker to lose his mind."

"Did you define 'lose his mind'? Because I'm in."

"The betting has closed," I tell her, and she scowls.

"Here." Suzie shoves Lizzie into Lexi's arms. "We'll be right back," she says before grabbing Grayson's hand and dragging him out of the room and down the hallway.

Lexi looks around in confusion. "What's going on?"

Faith clears her throat. "Um, I believe Lizzie is four weeks old today."

Lexi smiles down at the baby and I can't help but wish it was our baby she was smiling at. "Are you four weeks old? You're getting to be a big girl."

She drags her gaze away from the baby to respond to Faith. "I don't know what Lizzie being four weeks old has to do with Suzie and Grayson running out of here like a couple of school kids on summer break."

Faith blushes. "Well, you see…"

"The doctor gave her the okay for s-e-x today," Hailey explains.

A sparkle lights Lexi's eyes. "I bet Phoebe has her baby before they return."

"I'll take that bet," Wally says.

"Me too," I say together with Barney and Sid.

Lexi leans close. "What am I missing?"

Since the bets have already been made, I don't hesitate to tell her. "Grayson hasn't been with Suzie since she was eight months pregnant."

"Gotcha!"

Lizzie's little face scrunches together before she emits a loud fart. "Oh shit."

I bark out a laugh. "Shit is right." I stand and pick up the diaper bag from where Suzie dumped it. "Come on. Let's go change her."

"You're going to help?"

My chest constricts at her disbelief. I wish I was helping to change my own child's diaper, but I'll take what I can get. I force a smile on my face. "Sure will, Whiskey."

I lead her out of the room and down the hallway to a family bathroom. I click open the changing table, but Lexi remains frozen near the door. I step to her. "What's wrong?"

She bites her lip and stares at me for a moment before finally speaking, "I know you wanted children." I nod. I did. I do. "But if you marry me, we can't have children. After I lost Megan, I can't …" She gulps.

"Shh…" I hush her because I'm not making her talk about what happened. It's obviously still painful for her and I don't want Lexi to feel pain ever. "Yes, I realize we can't have biological children together."

Her eyebrow raises. "Biological children? Do you mean you want to adopt?"

I take Lizzie from her and place the baby on the changing table. "What would you say if I said yes?"

I chance a glance behind me to find her chewing on her bottom lip. "I don't know. I never thought about it."

I return my attention to the squirming baby in my hands and remove her diaper. I hand the soiled diaper to Lexi, and she hands me a wipe and fresh diaper. Damn. We work well as a team.

"Never thought about it as in it's a hard no? Or never thought about it and the idea is worth thinking about?"

"To be honest, I was thinking more about fostering."

My hands freeze. She's been thinking about it, too. I'm not alone in my yearning to have children.

"You're great with the kids you coach on the hockey team. It's obvious you make a difference in their lives. I thought …" She clears her throat. "Well, I thought if we can't have our own children, we could make the lives of those children who don't have the best home lives better."

I can't speak. I can barely breathe. I knew Lexi was perfect for me, but how is it she gets better and better every day?

"I mean if you prefer to adopt, I'm open to adoption as well, but I guess I kind of got swept away with the idea of helping kids…"

I finish changing Lizzie's diaper and pick her up before responding.

"I think it's a great idea. I know there are a ton of hoops we have to go through to become foster parents, but I'm up for the challenge if you are."

Her eyes sparkle with unshed tears. "I am totally up for the challenge."

I lean forward and kiss her nose. "It's decided then." We stand there smiling at each other for a few moments before she reaches down to grab the diaper bag.

"Damn," Barney swears when we enter the waiting room and slaps a bill in Wally's hand.

Wally chuckles. "They have a baby with them. You didn't seriously think they'd get busy in the family bathroom, did you?"

I feel Lexi's body tremble with silent laughter next to mine.

"Any news on Phoebe?" I ask since I have no intention of discussing my sex life with my brothers and their families.

"Ryker's holding on to his temper by a thread, Phoebe hasn't yelled at him once, and the nurse hasn't been by once to update us."

Mary Ann gets to her feet. "I'll go check."

She's barely out the door before Max asks his daughter, "When are you going to make me a grandfather?"

Hailey rears back. "Are you kidding me? I'm not ready for children. Besides, you're still raising Ollie."

"Ollie's a senior. He'll be out of the apartment soon. I want to hear the sound of pitter-patter."

Faith chokes at Max's words. "I'm not old enough to be a grandmother."

Meanwhile, Aiden looks ready to explode. I know he's been pushing Hailey to have his child since Suzie announced she was pregnant. He wants to give her a family, but she's not ready.

Mary Ann returns to announce, "It should be anytime now."

"How is Phoebe not screaming down the hallway?" Lexi asks.

"Someone is high as a kite right now, and it's not Ryker. Although, he could use a sedative."

With Phoebe in the hospital, Ryker would lose a limb before he'd accept any medication that would make him less than one-hundred percent alert. I've always considered myself a protector, but I've got nothing on him.

Lexi sits and I place the baby in her arms. I settle next to her to await the arrival of the next baby in our family.

Less than five minutes later, Ryker walks into the room carrying a tiny bundle wrapped in blue and appearing shell shocked. He clears his throat before announcing, "This is Connor Ryker Rossi."

Everyone stands to gather around the baby, but Ryker growls at anyone who gets too close. I surmise no one will be holding this baby but him and Phoebe for a while.

"Poor Phoebe, Connor looks exactly like Ryker. She's going to need a shotgun to keep the girls away once he hits puberty."

I chuckle at Lexi's announcement, but she's not wrong.

"Who hits puberty?" Suzie asks as she pushes her way to the front of the group. Her hair is a mess, and her lips are swollen. Meanwhile, behind her, Grayson is tucking his shirt into his pants.

"Guess I won the bet," Lexi sings as she hands Suzie her baby back.

I draw her near. "You might have won the bet, but I'm the lucky one," I whisper in her ear and watch with satisfaction as goosebumps appear on her skin. Oh yeah, I'm the winner here.

Chapter 36

We've been friends for so long, I can't remember which one of us is the bad influence.

TEN YEARS LATER

Hailey

I can't help but smile as I survey Val and Barney's backyard. The place is packed with all my favorite people. My pops and Faith as well as all my uncles and their partners plus all my friends and their children.

I plop down in a chair next to Suzie. "How are things, my favorite klutzy girl?"

She glares at me. "Don't say the k-word. Lydia thinks it's contagious."

I giggle. Suzie and her girls. She's got four of them now.

I watch as Aiden strolls over. I certainly got lucky when I married the handsome man, and he's only gotten better with age. His hair is as brown as ever, but he has spots of gray in his beard now. It's sexy as hell, although I still tease him about getting old.

"Here you go," he says and hands me a plate laden with food.

I smile in thanks before inhaling the scent of barbeque food. Ah, brats, potato salad, and … Blech! My stomach revolts at the smell of egg salad. I shove the plate back toward Aiden.

"There's something wrong with the egg salad."

Suzie giggles next to me. "There's nothing wrong with the egg salad. It's normal in your condition." She waggles her eyebrows.

Aiden halts. "Your condition. What's wrong with you? Are you sick? And why the hell does Suzie know before me?"

I glare at my *former* friend before standing and approaching Aiden with my hands up. "I'm not sick. And Suzie knows by accident."

"Right. Accident. Me running to the drugstore to pick up the test is an accident. Sure." Suzie just can't keep her mouth shut, can she?

Aiden's eyes light up. "Test?"

I grasp his hand. "Let's talk about this somewhere private."

"You might as well tell him here and now. Otherwise, we'll have to follow you into the house and listen behind the door."

I groan. I love my friends, but they've become even nosier as the years have gone by. Privacy amongst this group is a thing of the past.

"What's going on?" Pops grumbles as he and Faith join us. "Do you need me to kick Aiden's ass?"

It doesn't matter how long Aiden and I have been married, Pops still enjoys threatening to kick his ass on a regular occasion. "You like Aiden, remember Pops?"

He crosses his arms over his chest and glares at my husband. "Doesn't mean he can't use a good kick in the rear every once in a while."

Suzie claps. "This is awesome. Good news and we get a show of the silver fox and the sexy detective fighting. Can you remove your shirts first, please?"

Grayson arrives and claps a hand over her mouth. "Sorry. She'll be quiet now."

Yeah, good luck with that. As if he's been able to control Suzie since they've been married. Spoiler alert. He hasn't.

Aiden squeezes my hands. "Please, honey. Tell me what's wrong. Whatever it is we can deal with it. Is it—"

"Stop!" I yell at him before he can start listing a bunch of scary diseases. "I'm not sick. I'm pregnant."

His mouth falls open and his entire body seems to freeze. "D-d-did you say pregnant?"

"Yeah, lover boy," Suzie yells. Told you Grayson can't control her. "Your sperm and her egg—"

Aiden's whoop cuts her off. "We're having a baby!" He picks me up and twirls me around.

Pops growls at him. "Maybe you shouldn't twirl your wife – my daughter – around after she just announced she's pregnant."

Faith slaps him. "It's fine."

I ignore the scene around me. "Are you happy?"

"Are you kidding?" Aiden's eyes sparkle. "You've made me the happiest man in the world." His lips touch mine, and I thread my hands through his hair to draw him near.

"Stop making out with my daughter." Pops shoves his way between us and hauls me into his arms. "About damn time you make me a grandfather."

"Hey!" Phoebe shouts. "My kids call you grandpa."

"Someone's in trouble," I sing.

He releases me to deal with Phoebe, and Aiden claims me again.

"Thank you, honey. Thank you for building this beautiful life with me."

My eyes well with unshed tears. I swipe at them. "Damn pregnancy hormones."

"Yeah. We'll blame the hormones."

I slap him. "Shush. I want to see how Pops gets out of the mess he created."

Phoebe

"Darling," Pops squeezes my shoulder. "I'm sorry. I didn't mean to implicate your boys aren't my grandchildren."

I roll my eyes. "I know, but I thought Aiden and Hailey might want to celebrate their news in private." I point to where the couple is sneaking off.

He chuckles. "When did you become devious?"

I huff. "Since I have two boys, the oldest of whom is ten, but thinks he's a teenager."

"He got caught kissing a girl again?"

"Worse," I grump. "He got caught kissing two different girls on the same day at school."

Ryker throws his arm around my shoulders and pulls me close before kissing my hair. "Boys will be boys."

I slap his chest. "Don't you dare, big guy! Boys will be boys is an excuse that allows boys to do whatever they want. Our boys will learn to respect girls!"

He sighs. "They're ten and eight. They're not exactly impregnating their classmates."

"It's disrespectful how Connor runs around kissing all the girls he wants, and Axel looks up to his big brother like he's a rockstar," I tell him.

"You might want to invest in shares in whatever company makes condoms because our household will be buying a boatload of them," I say to Pops.

Ryker grasps my hand and draws me away from the crowd. Once we're in a secluded corner of the yard, he caresses my cheeks. "Princess, you need to calm down. Our boys are good. They're healthy and happy."

"They're also carousers at the tender ages of ten and eight. It's not okay, big guy." Tears threaten, but I'm on a roll. "I know how it feels to be abused by a predatory male. I refuse to let my boys become men who don't understand women are their equals."

"Fuck." He brushes the tears from my eyes. "I'll talk to them."

I raise an eyebrow. "Promise?"

"Of course."

"Good." I nod. "Because if you don't, I'm going back to work at *You Cheat, We Eat.* I'm sure Hailey could use my help now she's pregnant."

His nostrils flare. After an incident when a man chased me in my car and I ended up in an accident, Ryker put his foot down about me working – although it was totally not my fault. No more investigating insurance fraud, he insisted. Since we didn't need the money and I was exhausted from raising two boys and trying to work, I didn't put up too much of a fight. But now our boys are older and I'm getting anxious to get out of the house again.

"You win this round, Princess, but don't push it."

I bat my eyelashes at him. "Me? Push it?"

Suzie

Grayson growls before he stalks off. I survey the backyard to see what's got him all hot and bothered. Uh oh. Connor is kissing Lizzie. This won't end well. I rush after my husband.

"Stop, Grayson." I reach for him, but he's walking too fast for my short legs to keep up with his. "They're fine."

"What are you going to do about that?" he shouts at Ryker and points to Connor and Lizzie.

Ryker looks to where he's pointing and sighs when he notices the kids. "I got this."

"Are you sure?" Phoebe asks. "Hailey said my office is ready for me whenever I want to return to work."

What's she talking about? I thought she was happy being a stay-at-home mom.

We follow Ryker as he marches to the children. Connor notices us first. His eyes widen before he pulls away from Lizzie and shoves her behind him. My daughter isn't going to allow herself to be pushed away, though. She nudges Connor until she's standing next to him.

"Connor," Ryker begins.

The little guy raises his eyebrow and it's like looking through a time machine at Ryker twenty-five years ago. Phoebe's right. She needs to start stocking up on condoms soon.

I hold out my hand. "Lizzie, come here, please."

She sticks out her bottom lip and stomps her foot. "Why? I didn't do anything wrong."

"Did I say you did anything wrong?"

"Daddy has his 'I need to get my shotgun'-face."

Sigh. Her daddy does indeed have his shotgun face on.

"Why couldn't I have sons?" Grayson grumbles.

I act stricken. "You don't love our girls?"

Lizzie gets in on the act. "Don't you love us, Daddy?" She even bats her eyelashes.

Her sisters, Lydia, Catherine, and Mary join us. Catherine wraps herself around his left leg, while Mary wraps herself around his right leg. Lydia goes for his middle.

Grayson caresses their hair. "And you want another one of these?"

"Of course, I do. We still need a Jane."

Yes, I named my children after the Bennet sisters in *Pride and Prejudice.* I blame Hailey and her whole obsession with drama.

"You do realize we're not living in Victorian England?"

I roll my eyes. "Duh. I could hardly be the owner of an empire if we lived back then."

"An empire?"

"Beers from Shorty's Brewing Sensation are served in bars all across our nation. In fact, we just signed a deal to supply

American Family Field. You should know since you're the marketing manager."

Unlike Phoebe, I didn't quit working when I had my girls. It helps my husband doesn't disappear for days on end to catch the criminals of the world. Grayson and I are a team. We run the brewery together, and we raise our children together.

We agree on most things. Except for how to raise girls. He thinks he can keep our daughters protected and stop them from dating until they're twenty-five. Seeing as we just caught our ten-year-old hiding behind a tree kissing Connor, I think his ideas went up in smoke.

"What if we have a boy this time? You can't name a boy Jane."

"I think we've established by now you're incapable of making boys."

"Yeah, Daddy," Lizzie chimes in. "The male establishes the gender of the child."

"I want a sister," Mary says, although she has a hard time with the S and sister comes out sounding like fifter.

I love my girls.

Grayson tousles her hair. "But then you won't be the baby of the family."

"Me not a baby."

Before I can respond, a cheer goes up from the crowd. I glance over my shoulder to see our very own hero, Ollie, has arrived.

Faith

I frown when I note Ollie is not alone. Of course, he's not. My boy has turned into a womanizer.

"My son is a man whore. Where did I go wrong?"

Max pulls me close. "You didn't go wrong. He's not a man whore. He's merely sewing his oats before he settles down."

I have no problem my son isn't ready to settle down yet. He's only twenty-seven after all. But the casual hook-ups and different women on his arm every night? Those, I have problems with. And it's not the tabloids exaggerating his exploits either. I've seen it with my very own eyes.

After my early retirement, I convinced Max to slow down and stop slinging beer every night at McGraw's. Now, we spend part of the year following Ollie around as he travels for his soccer matches. I never expected to have a son who's a professional athlete, but he landed a soccer scholarship to college, and it all kind of exploded from there.

Ollie swaggers toward me dragging the woman behind him. "Hey, Ma." He leans down to kiss my cheek. "I have someone I want to introduce you to."

He clears his throat. "This is Cora."

I study the woman next to him. She doesn't resemble his usual conquests. She's dressed conservatively in a long skirt for one. Her face is also fresh and free of make-up.

I extend my hand. "Hi, Cora. I'm Faith and this is my husband Max."

"Nice to meet you, Mr. and Mrs. McGraw."

Polite as well. What is going on here?

"Here, he is. Our hero," Wally shouts before engulfing Ollie in a hug. The rest of the brothers clap him on the back.

Ollie blushes. "I'm no hero."

Wally winks and glances toward Cora. "That's not what I've heard."

Ollie growls and pulls Cora near. "Stop."

Hailey shoves her way through the crowd. "Ollie! Ollie! Ollie!" She throws herself at him and he catches her.

Aiden growls and pulls her off of him. "You need to be careful in your condition."

"My condition? I thought we established we're not living in Victorian England."

Ollie looks back and forth between them before a smile stretches across his face. "Sis, are you finally making me an uncle?"

She giggles in response, and Ollie whoops before reaching for her again. Aiden stands in his way. "Be careful, you big oaf."

Cora tugs on the bottom of Ollie's t-shirt. "Maybe I should go and let you celebrate with your family."

Ollie uses her hand to pull her near. "You're not going anywhere."

"But—"

"I'll introduce you to everyone. Don't worry. Everyone will be nice to you."

The poor girl is practically trembling in fright. I step in. "Cora, would you mind helping me in the kitchen?"

I don't need help in the kitchen, but I'll think of something. Plus, it will give me a chance to get a feel for this girl my boy appears to be smitten with.

"Ma," Ollie grumbles.

I round my eyes. "What?"

He frowns but maneuvers Cora until she's standing in front of him. "You going to be okay alone with my mother?"

"Why? She's not going to kill me and use my skin to make a lampshade, is she?"

Thank goodness. The girl does have a backbone.

"I promise it will be the most beautiful lampshade you've ever seen. I may even add fringe and tassels," I tell her.

"Fringe and tassels? You sound like my grandmother."

"Burn!" Ollie shouts, but he pushes her toward me while mouthing *be nice.* I roll my eyes. I'm always nice. It's practically my middle name.

Chrissie

I watch Faith escort Cora into the house. "Who would have thought Ollie would end up with a shy girl?"

"Considering the rest of the women in this family, she's never going to get a word in edgewise."

I slap Wally's arm. "You make us sound like a bunch of heathens."

"Angel, you catch criminals for a living. It's the very definition of heathen."

"No, it's not," Suzie proclaims. "A heathen is a person who doesn't belong to a widely held religion."

Hailey sighs. "I love how you only know the proper definition of a word when it suits you."

Suzie starts to protest, but Hailey raises her hand to stop her. "Not now, Shorty. I need to have a discussion with Chrissie."

I cross my arms over my chest and stare down at Hailey. She's a mere two inches shorter than me, but I know it intimidates the hell out of her when I stare at her, which means I do it as often as I possibly can, of course.

"Eek! Don't give me the stare. I just wanted—"

"To ask me about spending more time in the office now you're pregnant," I finish.

Suzie punches her fist into the air. "I told you Chrissie can read minds!"

I ignore her to ask Wally, "What do you think?"

I'm not asking my husband because I'm some kept woman. Please. As if. I'm asking him because we're partners as in business partners. Wally never did get around to becoming a woodworker. He missed the thrill of the chase too much. He ended up getting his PI license as well, and now we investigate cases together.

He shrugs in response to my question. "It might be good to slow down some."

Those are not the words I ever expected to hear him say. Wally may be nearing seventy now, but he hasn't slowed down – much. He's still fitter than most men in their thirties.

"You won't get bored?"

He shrugs. "I still have all the woodworking equipment."

I snort. "I know. It's gathering dust in the shed you built in my backyard."

He palms my neck and draws me near. "*Our* backyard. You'd think after ten years of marriage, you'd understand what's mine is yours."

"I'm still getting used to the idea," I tease.

"You need me to prove you're mine?"

"Maybe."

Hailey groans. "Oh no. Uncle Wally and Aunt Chrissie are going to go at it in public again."

You get caught with your pants down one time. "It wasn't in public."

"The door wasn't locked. Same thing."

"Maybe you should learn to knock before entering a room."

"I thought you and Wally were super-secret spies who would know I was coming."

I smirk, and she squirms. "And how did that work out for you?"

Valerie

"What are you talking about? How did I miss this?" My gaze ping pongs between Chrissie and Hailey. "Please tell me I didn't miss out on Chrissie and Wally having a rumble in the hay at the office."

Hailey feigns gagging. "You do realize you're talking about my aunt and uncle. Gross."

I roll my eyes. "Oh, please. It's not like you're some lily-white, squeaky clean angel. You're pregnant."

"Now, now, Trouble." Barney hugs my waist. "We've discussed this. My niece is pure as the driven snow."

I snort. "And I suppose she's pregnant via immaculate conception."

"How was your trip to Finland, Aunt Val?" Hailey asks, and I narrow my eyes on her. She knows how much I love to talk about the trips Barney takes me on. Does she think she can derail me away from the topic of Wally and Chrissie's sex life?

"Yeah, Val. How was your trip, you lady of leisure?"

As if Faith is one to talk. We retired on practically the same day, but instead of following my son all over America as he takes the soccer world by storm, I've been traveling the world with Barney.

"Did you know public nudity is not a crime in Finland?"

I have no idea if this is true. I'm doing what I always do – stirring up trouble.

"You have got to tell me how you know this! Did you get caught with your pants down? Like, literally, your pants were around your ankles. Or did you stay at a nudist colony? Grayson, we're going to Finland on our next vacation!"

"I thought you wanted to have another baby. We can't afford to travel with five girls to Europe."

"I guess I forgot to tell you about the call from Wrigley Field."

"You what?" Grayson marches over, grabs Suzie's hand, and leads her away. "Excuse us."

Mary Ann frowns at Sid. "Why don't you ever take me anywhere? Max and Faith are traveling the country and Barney and Val galivant around the world and yet you never take me anywhere."

"Woman," Sid growls. "I took you on a three-week cruise in the Caribbean."

"Yeah. Last year. Where have we gone this year? Huh?"

I butt into their discussion to say, "Barney's already got our next trip planned."

Mary Ann throws her arms in the air before marching off with Sid chasing after her.

I can feel Barney's silent laughter against my side. "And here I thought I'd have to come up with another nickname for you at some point, *Trouble.*"

"You did? What gave you the idea I would ever give up my troublemaking ways? My suggestion of joining the mile-high club on our return flight? Or maybe it was when I put the mini bottles of liquor from the hotel in my bag and we drank them all while taking the dogsled tour?"

"Not your best idea."

"I'm not the one who decided to mix the gin and tequila. Who mixes gin and tequila?"

I was fine but someone got a bit of 'motion sickness'. Ha! Right. Motion sickness. Barney hasn't had motion sickness a day in his life. Someone was drunk off his ass is what happened.

"Who wants to watch a slide presentation of our latest trip?"

Lexi

Toby, our fifteen-year-old foster, groans. "Not another slide presentation."

Before I have a chance to yell at him, Lenny reprimands him. "You will respect your elders."

Jeremy, our eight-year-old foster, runs over. "Mama Lexi. Mama Lexi."

I sweep him into my arms. "What is it, little one?"

He points at Suzie's middle child. "Lydia called me a bad name."

Knowing Suzie, I'm almost afraid to ask. "What did she call you?"

"A bastard."

Before I can speak, Suzie raises her hands. "I'll deal with it. Lydia," she bellows, "get your bottom over here."

Lydia skips over to us; not appearing the least bit guilty.

"Did you call Jeremy a name?" Suzie asks. At Lydia's nod, she asks her, "What did you call him?"

"A bastard."

I hug Jeremy tight at the nasty word. It's true the boy was born out of wedlock, but bastard is simply a nasty word, and no one should call a child of a single mother one.

Suzie kneels down in front of her daughter. "Do you know what bastard means?"

Lydia nods. "Of course. It means male cousin. Jeremy is my cousin, isn't he? He's Aunt Lexi's son. Thus, cousin."

Suzie pats her head. "Yes, Jeremy is your cousin. Who told you what the word bastard means?"

"Cousin Connor."

"Ryker!" Phoebe shouts. "Our boys are going to military school." She marches after her husband as they hunt for their oldest son.

Suzie hugs her daughter. "We need to have a little lesson about believing whatever your cousin tells you."

Jeremy squirms to be let down. "Can I go play?" I nod, and he seizes Lydia's hand before the two run off together.

"May I be excused?" Toby asks.

I feel bad for him. He's five years older than the oldest kids here. And five years is a lot when you're talking about the difference between a ten-year-old and a teenager. I hand him his phone.

"Here."

"Thanks, Mama Lexi," he shouts as he walks into the house. Probably to find some privacy to call his girlfriend.

"Phoebe's not the only one who needs to stock up on condoms," I grumble as I watch him leave.

Lenny squeezes my shoulder. "Already done. And we've had the talk about respecting the fairer sex, too."

"The fairer sex? Please tell me you didn't say fairer sex to him, old man."

He tweaks my nose. "Don't be a brat, Whiskey."

I waggle my eyes at him. "Why not? You gonna tie me up if I misbehave?"

He growls and steps closer. "All you have to do is ask."

"What are you waiting for?"

"Thank you."

"For what? I'm pretty sure I enjoy being tied up about as much as you enjoy tying me up."

He smirks. "Oh, I know you enjoy it more, but I wasn't talking about that. I was thanking you for giving me a beautiful life."

I melt into him. "It's you who has given me a beautiful life."

His lips touch my forehead. "Agree to disagree."

About the Author

D.E. Haggerty is an American who has spent the majority of her adult life abroad. She has lived in Istanbul, various places throughout Germany, and currently finds herself in The Hague. She has been a military policewoman, a lawyer, a B&B owner/operator and now a writer.